"Eden?" Ror

He couldn't lose her. He just couldn't.

"Here," she finally said. Like him, her breathing was labored, but he could pinpoint her location in the stall next to him.

Rory used his hand to try to wave away some of the cloudy debris particles that were obstructing his vision, and stepping over some of the pieces of shattered wood, he inched his way to the stall.

And he saw Eden.

Alive.

The relief flooded through him. In the back of his mind, Rory realized the crime scene had been blown to hell and back and that the killer was likely responsible. But he couldn't focus on that now. He went to Eden, and before he could stop himself, he pulled her into his arms.

She didn't resist.

DEPUTIES UNDER FIRE

DELORES FOSSEN

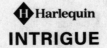

INTRIGUE

If you purchased this book without a cover you should be aware that this book is stolen property. It was reported as "unsold and destroyed" to the publisher, and neither the author nor the publisher has received any payment for this "stripped book."

ISBN-13: 978-1-335-69018-0

Deputies Under Fire

Copyright © 2025 by Delores Fossen

All rights reserved. No part of this book may be used or reproduced in any manner whatsoever without written permission.

Without limiting the author's and publisher's exclusive rights, any unauthorized use of this publication to train generative artificial intelligence (AI) technologies is expressly prohibited.

This is a work of fiction. Names, characters, places and incidents are either the product of the author's imagination or are used fictitiously. Any resemblance to actual persons, living or dead, businesses, companies, events or locales is entirely coincidental.

For questions and comments about the quality of this book, please contact us at CustomerService@Harlequin.com.

TM and ® are trademarks of Harlequin Enterprises ULC.

 Harlequin Enterprises ULC
22 Adelaide St. West, 41st Floor
Toronto, Ontario M5H 4E3, Canada
www.Harlequin.com

Printed in Lithuania

Delores Fossen, a *USA TODAY* bestselling author, has written over a hundred and fifty novels, with millions of copies of her books in print worldwide. She's received a Booksellers' Best Award and an RT Reviewers' Choice Best Book Award. She was also a finalist for a prestigious RITA® Award. You can contact the author through her website at www.deloresfossen.com.

Books by Delores Fossen

Harlequin Intrigue

Renegade Canyon

Her Baby, Her Badge
Deputies Under Fire

Saddle Ridge Justice

The Sheriff's Baby
Protecting the Newborn
Tracking Down the Lawman's Son
Child in Jeopardy

Silver Creek Lawman: Second Generation

Targeted in Silver Creek
Maverick Detective Dad
Last Seen in Silver Creek
Marked for Revenge

The Law in Lubbock County

Sheriff in the Saddle
Maverick Justice
Lawman to the Core
Spurred to Justice

Visit the Author Profile page at Harlequin.com.

CAST OF CHARACTERS

Deputy Rory McClennan—When someone targets his father's enemies, Rory and his ex, Eden Gallagher, end up on the killer's hit list.

Deputy Eden Gallagher—She'll do whatever it takes to protect Rory and her son, and stop a killer from claiming everyone and everything she loves.

Tyler McClennan—Eden and Rory's nine-month-old son. He has no idea of the danger, and Rory and Eden plan to keep him out of harm's way.

Ike McClennan—Rory's cruel, domineering father, who comes under suspicion when his enemies start turning up dead, but Ike is adamant that someone is setting him up.

Frank Mott—A local rancher who's had a long-standing feud with Ike. Just how far would he go to get revenge?

Diedre Bennington—Ike's former lover. After she ended her relationship with Ike, he set out to ruin her, and Diedre could be the one who's setting him up to take the fall for the murder.

Helen Weatherford—The sister of Ike's late wife, and she blames Ike for her sister's death. She admits she'd do anything to destroy Ike, but does that include murder?

Chapter One

It was like stepping into hell.

The memories immediately slammed into Deputy Eden Gallagher. The stench of the mold and decay in the barn. The dank chill crawling over her skin. The autumn wind moaning through the cracks in what was left of the walls.

And the still-dark stain on the cracked concrete floor.

Once, it'd been more than a stain.

It'd been fresh blood, and there had been a body, too.

"Mellie," she muttered, not able to suppress saying the name of the woman who'd been her mother in every single way that mattered.

Five months wasn't nearly long enough for the grief to have passed. Or for the memories of seeing Mellie's body not to cause a jolt inside her.

"You don't have to be here," her fellow deputy, Rory McClennan, insisted. "I can call in someone else."

Except he was more than her fellow deputy. A whole lot more. Rory was technically her boss at Renegade Canyon PD since he was the acting sheriff while Sheriff Grace Granger was on maternity leave.

Rory was also the father of her nine-month-old son, Tyler.

So, yes, a whole lot more.

Even though Rory and she weren't a couple any longer, and they hadn't been since before Tyler had been born, he wouldn't have any trouble realizing that she was far from okay. He was well aware this place held the hellish memories that were causing her breath to go thin and her heartbeat to race.

"It's my shift," she said, barely managing to get out the words. "I can do my job."

She hoped.

For Rory to call in someone else, it would mean a deputy would end up coming in on their night off. That was because only Rory, Bennie Whitt and she worked the swing shift, 4:00 p.m. to midnight, and Bennie was manning the office. She and Rory had opted for the swing shift so they could spend a good portion of the day with their son, and while those hours were generally quiet in their hometown, that hadn't been the case tonight.

A call had come in at nine thirty, forty minutes earlier, through Dispatch. A frantic ranch owner, Fran Cagel, had said her golden retriever had come home with blood on its feet and fur. According to Fran, the dog often came to the old barn since it was only a couple of acres away from her ranch.

Of course, it was entirely possible that the retriever had gone elsewhere since he'd been off-leash and roaming, as Fran had said was his routine. But after Rory and Eden had used a simple test to confirm it was indeed blood on the dog, they'd arranged for the sample to be picked up by the county lab to see if it was human. They had also contacted the town hospital in case someone injured showed up.

So far, nothing from the hospital, and while waiting for the lab results, they'd come here.

To hell.

To the place where Mellie had died. Or rather, where her body had been dumped.

Since they didn't know who'd killed her, or why, that only added to the nightmarish memories. It was bad enough when someone was murdered, but it was worse when there was no justice.

Especially when Eden was in the business of getting justice.

That failure had given her plenty of sleepless nights.

"Let's just get this done," Eden insisted, a reminder to herself to get her focus back on the job.

This should be a quick in-and-out, where they could determine if the blood had indeed come from here. If it hadn't, then they could search the surrounding area. But since it was already dark and the barn was out in the sticks, it'd be morning before a search team could start.

Stepping over the spot where Mellie had been found, she and Rory fanned their flashlights around the barn. It had probably once been impressive, with its massive arched top window above the entrance and the twelve stalls, six on each side. The glass was now broken, the remaining bits hanging on to the frame like loose, jagged teeth. And the rest of the place, well, there was nothing impressive about it.

"This should have been torn down years ago," Rory muttered.

Eden made a sound of agreement. If it had been, then Mellie wouldn't have been dumped here. Of course, that wouldn't have stopped her from dying, but at least she wouldn't have ended up here in this rot.

"I'll make another request," Eden assured him. Though her previous request had generated no results.

Seventy or so years ago, when the barn had first been

built, the owner had stalled prize palominos here. After the owner had passed away, the land—and therefore, the barn and the nearby house—had gone to a distant relative, who apparently had no desire to sell or maintain the property. The house had had been struck by lightning and caught on fire when Eden had been thirteen, twenty years ago, and because of the sinister look to the place, some of the local teenagers had dubbed it the Devil's Hideout.

After Mellie's body had been discovered, Eden had requested that the barn be destroyed since it could be a hazard, but the owner's lawyers had come back with the argument that it was on private land with clearly posted No Trespassing signs. Added to that, it was nearly a mile from a main road, and the only way for someone to reach it was via a rugged ranch trail.

All of that was true, and she had firsthand knowledge of the trail's ruggedness since that's how she and Rory had gotten here. But Eden wished there wasn't such a hellish visual reminder of her foster mother's murder.

Trying to shove aside that thought, Eden walked several feet into the barn, and with Rory right by her side, they paused to listen for anyone or any sounds that shouldn't be there.

Nothing.

So they shifted, Rory aiming his flashlight to the left while she fanned hers to the right. The flashlights were solid, but they weren't creating nearly enough illumination for her to see what was in the shadows.

And there were plenty of shadows.

"I don't see any blood or dog tracks on the floor," Rory whispered.

Neither did she, but the wind wasn't cooperating with their search. Along with creating those eerie whistling sounds, it was blowing around the dead leaves, dirt and other debris on the floor. There were fast-food bags, empty beer cans and even the remnants of what appeared to be a campfire in a banged-up metal bucket.

Judging from the talk she'd heard, the barn had become a ghoulish thrill for some teens. It was yet another reason to have it torn down.

Rory tipped his head toward the stalls. "We'll have to check them all."

Yes, they would, and there suddenly seemed like more than a dozen of them. Some still had stall doors. Others were just collapsed heaps of old wood. But each space needed to be searched, especially since there were enough large holes in the exterior walls, and the retriever could have gone in and out through one of those.

The two of them moved together, in a rhythm that came surprisingly easy considering they had only been working together for five months. Before that, she'd been a detective in SVU at San Antonio PD, where the pace was a whole lot different than here in her hometown. Still, after Mellie's death, Eden had felt the need to come home. The need to be part of the police force that was investigating her murder.

Of course, Rory had played into that decision, too.

They weren't a couple, not any longer, but he was Tyler's father, and despite her turbulent past with Rory and his powerful, corrupt father, Eden hadn't wanted to deny her son a chance to be with his dad.

Something that she hadn't had growing up.

That, and her birth mother's untimely death, had been the reason Eden had ended up in foster care on the Horseshoe Ranch in Renegade Canyon.

They kept moving. Kept looking. Kept listening. Still

no sign of blood or a body. Eden froze, though, when she saw a heap in the corner of one of the stalls.

She didn't say anything, but Rory must have sensed something was wrong because he shifted in that direction, automatically aiming his flashlight at the pile...of something. Whatever it was, it'd been covered with what appeared to be a ratty sleeping bag.

Glancing around, they went closer, and using the toe of his boot, Rory moved the sleeping bag aside. The tightness in her chest eased up when she saw it was a couple of pillows. Apparently, someone had been camping out. Maybe a teen—

Eden gasped when her phone vibrated in her pocket. That reaction was proof of just how on edge her nerves were. She yanked out her cell and breathed a whole lot easier when she saw it was a picture from the live-in nanny, Leslie Darrington.

She turned her phone so that Rory could see the sweet photo of Tyler asleep in his crib.

Night, night, Mommy and Daddy, Leslie had texted.

Despite her surroundings, Eden smiled and touched her fingers to the image of that precious little face. She and Rory might be at odds with each other, but there was no doubt they both loved their little boy.

Rory smiled, too, and for just a second, their gazes met. And for that second, the old heat was there.

No. No. No.

When was that blasted attraction finally going to cool down? Eden had to consider the answer to that was never. After all, Rory and she had been on and off since high school, and while their *on* time had been amazing, his father, Ike, had always found a way to tear them apart, along with making Mellie's life a living hell. It was hard to try being happy with Rory when Mellie had been suffering.

Eden took one last look at the photo and put her phone away. Just then, Rory's phone dinged with a text. He looked at the screen and definitely didn't have the same smiling reaction that he'd had seeing Tyler's photo.

"It's from the county lab," he explained. "The blood on the dog is human."

Eden groaned and squeezed her eyes shut for a moment. That was not what she'd wanted to hear, even though the presence of blood didn't mean someone had been killed. She wanted to cling to the hope that someone, maybe the person who'd been camping out in that sleeping bag, had injured himself and left a blood trail for the dog to trample through.

"They'll run it through the database to see if they get a hit," Rory added a moment later.

Good. But Eden knew the limits of the database. The majority of people weren't even in it unless they'd committed a crime or worked in a job, like as a cop, that required a sample of their DNA to be on file. Still, it was possible they'd be able to get a match so they'd know whom they were looking for.

He slipped his phone back in his pocket, and they resumed the search. Eden got another jolt when a rat skittered across the floor right in front of them. She was silently cursing it when she heard something. A moan, maybe? Or maybe just the wind.

Rory must have heard it, too, because he stopped, and they both turned in the direction of where the sound had come from.

The very last stall.

They moved toward it, quickening their pace but still

making cursory glances inside the stalls they passed along the way.

The sound came again. Definitely not the wind, and it caused them to move even faster. When they reached the stall, they aimed their flashlights inside.

At first, Eden didn't see anything. Not until she directed the light over the far right corner.

Then, she spotted her.

A woman.

Oh, mercy. And she was covered with blood.

"I'll call for an ambulance," Rory said, snatching out his phone.

Eden hurried to the woman, and she stooped down so she could check for a pulse. It was weak, but she was alive. She had also obviously lost a lot of blood. It wasn't just on her face and clothes, but had pooled around her.

The woman lifted her eyelids, barely, moaned again and shivered. "Help me," she murmured, her voice barely audible.

"We will," Eden assured her. "Who are you?" she asked.

No response, and her eyelids drifted back down.

Eden studied her, taking in the long blond hair, what she could see of it, anyway. The torn black skirt, red top and heels. The clothing looked expensive.

And those stab wounds looked lethal.

Since adding pressure to the wounds could do more harm than good and potentially cause internal injuries, Eden focused on what little she could do. She yanked off her jacket and draped it over the woman to stave off what had to be a chill from the shock of the blood loss.

Behind her, she heard Rory finishing that 911 call for the ambulance, while she checked for any obstructions in the woman's airway. There weren't any. And the blood on her face and hair appeared to have come from a cut on the scalp. Maybe a sign of some kind of blunt-force trauma.

"An ambulance is on the way," Rory informed her, and he came into the stall, kneeling down beside the woman.

"Who did this to you?" Eden asked her, hoping this time she would get an answer.

But the woman made no sound.

However, Rory did. He groaned, causing Eden to snap back toward him.

"Hell," Rory muttered. "I know her."

There was something in his voice, in his stark expression, that had Eden dreading what he would say next.

"She's Brenda Watford," he added.

Eden repeated the name a couple of times, but she had to shake her head. It didn't ring any bells. "How do you know her?"

He swallowed hard. "She's, uh, my father's girlfriend. Ex-girlfriend," Rory amended. "And the last time I saw Brenda, Ike was threatening to kill her."

Chapter Two

Hell.

That was the one word that kept repeating through Rory's head. And he was certain it would keep repeating as the night dragged on.

A woman was now unconscious and barely clinging to life. His father's ex-girlfriend. Rory would need answers about that. Answers, too, as to why Brenda had been left here in this barn, where Mellie's body had been found.

Were the two attacks connected?

The odds were yes, they were. It was too much of a coincidence for it to be otherwise. And that meant the connection would lead straight back to his father, Ike.

So, yeah.

That *hell* would be echoing in his head for a while.

With Eden right by his side, Rory kept watch around them as the EMTs eased Brenda into the ambulance. The moment they had her secured inside, they hit the sirens and started for the hospital.

Fast.

Because every second was going to count now. The woman was hanging on by a thread.

He and Eden hurried to the cruiser that they'd left off the old ranch trail and jumped in so they could follow. If they got lucky, Brenda would regain consciousness and be able to tell them who'd attacked her and put her in the barn. If she named his father... But Rory stopped and decided he'd cross that bridge once he came to it.

For now, he drove toward the Renegade Canyon Hospital, glancing around to see if there were any indications of who'd brought Brenda here. The CSIs would arrive soon and do a thorough check, but the scene had already been disturbed, first with Eden's and his arrival, and then with the EMTs and ambulance. Maybe potential evidence hadn't been destroyed that would help them ID Brenda's attacker.

He glanced at Eden, who was pulling up some info on her phone, and he saw the slight tremble in her hands. A tremble she wouldn't want him to notice. She was a tough cop.

A damn good one, too.

But that didn't mean she could tamp down the basic human emotion of grief. She'd basically just relived one of her worst nightmares by walking into the barn and seeing another bleeding woman. At least this time the woman was alive. That hadn't been the case with Mellie.

"I figure you're about to ask me if I'm okay," Eden murmured while the cruiser bobbled over the seriously uneven surface of the ranch trail. "Please don't, and I won't ask you the same."

Good. Because neither of them was anywhere in the *okay* range right now. She was fighting those traumatic memories, and he was dealing with the firestorm he was about to face. He got started on that firestorm by giving the voice command to make a call to his father.

As usual, Rory had to steel himself for any kind of contact with his dad. Things hadn't been civil between them for a long time.

Rory supposed if he had to put his finger on when the rift started, it would have been when his mother transferred ownership of the ranch to Rory's older brother, Dutton, when he turned twenty-one. Rory had been just sixteen then, but he'd had no trouble choosing his brother's side over their father's.

Ike hadn't taken that well at all.

Of course, Rory had known that Ike could be a vindictive, mean-as-a-snake SOB. Those traits hadn't improved over the years, and they'd escalated big-time when Rory had become a cop. Then, Ike's venom had gone up even more when Rory's mom had died nearly a year ago.

And again, when Eden had given birth to Rory's baby.

Ike hadn't learned that news until the day Eden had given birth since neither Eden nor Rory had felt the need to tell him sooner. No way did Ike approve of Rory having a baby with one of Mellie's foster-home kids. Or "brats," as Ike was fond of calling them.

The call to his father connected, and it rang and rang and rang. Just when Rory thought it would go to voice mail, Ike finally answered. "What the hell do you want?" he snarled, obviously seeing Rory's number on his caller ID.

"I need you to come into the police station," Rory answered, making sure he sounded exactly like the cop that he was. "Be there in one hour."

That should give him enough time to check on Brenda, arrange for a reserve deputy to guard her, get a search warrant for Ike's house and vehicles and then prep for what would be the interview from hell.

Ike laughed, and it wasn't from humor. "And why would I do that?"

"Because someone tried to kill Brenda Watford. She's alive and talking." Yeah, the last part was a lie, but he wanted to rattle Ike. Or rather, it would rattle him if he'd been the one who had actually attacked her. "Be at the police station in one hour, or I'll be out to arrest you."

With that, Rory ended the call, figuring that Ike might just try to ring him right back. He didn't. So he was probably calling his lawyer instead or trying to find out anything he could about Brenda's condition.

"I'll text the hospital chief to put a lid on any and everything about Brenda's condition. Or anything she might say if she regains consciousness," Eden explained, already typing the message. "You know Ike will probably show up there."

"I know," he agreed.

No way would he let Ike get anywhere near Brenda, but it would mean a showdown of sorts at the hospital. Then again, just about every face-to-face meeting with his father qualified as a showdown.

Rory heard the swooshing sound to indicate she'd sent the text to the hospital, and Eden continued typing on her phone. Like him, she was also keeping check around them in case Brenda's attacker was still in the area.

But there were no signs of anyone or anything out of the ordinary.

"All right, here's the background on Brenda," Eden said, reading from the report she'd obviously just accessed. "Brenda Elise Watford, no police record. Owner of Watford Real Estate in San Antonio. Blond hair and blue eyes. Five-three, one hundred and twenty pounds, according to her driver's license. Divorced, no kids. Aged forty-one." She stopped, looked at him. "That's a big age difference between Ike and her. Ike's what…seventy?"

Rory nodded. "He will be in a few weeks."

But it was hard for him to think of Ike as a senior citizen since he was a big, imposing man who still had a lot of muscle on him. Ike was plenty strong enough to have lifted a woman Brenda's size and carried her into that barn. Then again, Brenda could have been lured there and attacked, which would have meant that no carrying had been involved.

"Ike's girlfriends are usually a lot younger than he is," Rory added on to that. "And, yes, he had those girlfriends even when he was married to my mom. His relationships don't last long, though, because the women seem to grasp his true colors soon enough and dump him."

She stayed quiet a moment. "You said the last time you saw Brenda that Ike threatened to kill her."

Rory had known this was coming, and what he had to add to that comment was going to make Ike look even guiltier. "About six weeks ago, I went to the ranch to visit Dutton."

No need for him to explain that while Dutton owned Towering Oaks, he didn't live in the main house. Dutton had had his own place built, and it was as far away from Ike as possible, while still remaining on the actual ranch.

"I have to drive past the main house to get to Dutton's," Rory went on, "and that day, I saw Ike and Brenda in the driveway. They were clearly arguing, and I stopped when I saw Brenda slap and push him."

That put some fresh alarm on Eden's face. "Did Ike slap and push her back?"

"Not that I saw. But I don't know exactly what went on before I arrived." He paused, gathered his breath. "Ike told me to get lost." Of course, his father had added a lot of profanity to go along with that barked order. "I stayed put and talked to Brenda. She was fuming and said that Ike was turning her clients against her, that he was doing a smear campaign to ruin her name and that he'd even leaked some risqué photos of her on the internet."

"Did he?" Eden asked.

"Someone did. Brenda was in her underwear, doing what I guess you'd call a drunken sexy dance. Maybe for Ike." Though Rory definitely didn't like to think about that. "Maybe for someone else. But Brenda was convinced Ike had been the one to post them. I didn't get the chance to question her more on that because Ike and she got into a shouting match with some name calling and threats."

"Threats?" Eden repeated. "Like Ike saying he would kill her?"

"That and other things. Brenda said she was going to start her own smear campaign and that when she was done with him, Ike would regret he'd ever met her." Rory recalled the rage he'd seen on the woman's face. Then again, there had been fury on Ike's face, too. "That's when Ike said she'd better back off or she'd end up dead."

Eden didn't seem the least bit surprised by that. Then again, she'd heard Ike issue similar threats to Mellie when they'd gotten into disputes, usually when Ike accused one of Mellie's *brats* of trespassing on the ranch. Of course, the irony was Ike didn't own the ranch, and Dutton would have never caved to file trespassing charges against anyone in the foster home.

"Did Brenda back off?" Eden asked.

"I'm not sure." Hopefully, that was something they'd soon find out from the woman herself.

They finally reached the end of the trail and got onto the main road. The ambulance was able to pick up some speed. So was Rory, and he knew it wouldn't be long now before they reached the hospital.

"All right," Eden said, typing on her phone. "I'll start a deep dive on Brenda and go through all her social media."

That was one of Eden's specialties—data mining to come up with info and insights into victims, suspects and persons of interest. She'd no doubt honed that skill while working as a detective at SAPD, but she'd also developed some solid investigative expertise there as well.

And she would go at Ike with both barrels loaded.

Not literally. Eden wouldn't get violent with him, but she would dig, and dig hard, to prove Ike was responsible for the attack on Brenda. Because if he had indeed done it, that might also lead to his arrest for Mellie's murder. Not being able to solve that had no doubt been a constant, painful thorn in her side.

In his, too.

There'd been no physical evidence to tie Ike or anyone else to her death. Ike had been home alone at the time so he had no alibi, but there was also no proof that he'd gone out that night. The CSIs hadn't been able to find squat to get justice for a good woman who'd devoted her life to helping kids.

So, yeah, a thorn in his side as well.

"I'm not seeing any photos or posts about Ike on Brenda's Facebook page," Eden muttered. "She probably deleted them, but once I'm back at the station, I'll see if I can recover anything useful."

Ike wasn't on social media, so Eden wouldn't have that available to her, and while the ranch was sometimes in the news for its prize horses, Ike wasn't usually included in those articles. His father had basically washed his hands of the ranch and his sons. But for reasons Rory would never understand, he continued to live there. So did Ike's much younger brother and his wife, Asher and Kitty, and their twelve-year-old adopted daughter, Jamie. Jamie was one of the few people who Ike actually seemed to like and vice versa.

Rory hoped like hell that she wasn't in danger.

He made a mental note to talk to Asher, Kitty and Jamie about maybe staying elsewhere until the dust had settled on this investigation. Rory didn't think they were in actual danger, but Ike was a bear to be around during the best of times. No way were the *best of times* happening with him currently as their number-one murder suspect.

Rory drove past the Welcome to Renegade Canyon sign and continued to follow the ambulance onto Main Street and then into the parking lot of the hospital. The EMTs had obviously already alerted the medical staff, because the moment the ambulance pulled to a stop, two nurses and a doctor came rushing out.

Since there were very few degrees of separation in a small town, Rory recognized all of them and knew they weren't a threat to Brenda's safety. They were fast and efficient in working with the EMTs to get Brenda out of the ambulance, and she was then rushed not toward a treatment room, but straight toward the critical-care area.

Rory took out his phone to text Dispatch to get a reserve deputy here, and he went to the hall to wait for the EMTs to return so he could question them. If Brenda had regained consciousness in the ambulance, he wanted to know everything she'd said. However, he saw someone who had him stopping cold. The tall brunette was making a beeline toward him.

His aunt, Helen Weatherford.

She was his late mother's younger sister, and while she'd been raised in Renegade Canyon, she hadn't lived here since she left years ago for college. She now made her home in San Antonio.

Helen was wearing black jogging pants, a workout top and running shoes. As usual, she had her long hair pulled up into a ponytail. She looked like an AARP ad for a super fit fiftysomething-year-old woman.

"What are you doing here?" Rory asked, trying not to sound as if it was an accusation. Though that's exactly what it was.

Helen got closer and gave a rather frosty nonverbal greeting to him. Frosty because his aunt believed Ike, Dutton and he hadn't done enough to save her sister. And Rory had to admit he did feel some serious guilt about that. He simply hadn't realized just how serious his mother's illness was until it'd been too late.

"I was visiting an old friend. Sheila Mendoza," Helen said, her tone as icy as her expression. "She's recovering from an appendectomy."

Rory was sure he frowned. And that he looked confused. He didn't recall Helen being especially close friends with Sheila, and it was late. Well, late for hospital visits, anyway.

"Why are you here?" Helen asked, volleying glances at Eden and him. Her attention settled on the blood that was on Eden's shirt. "There's nothing wrong with your baby, is there?"

"No, Tyler's fine," Eden replied. "We're here on police business."

Helen made a sound that could have meant anything. "How's Dutton and his new baby?" she asked, but there didn't appear to be any real interest in her question. Dutton was clearly still on her bad side, too.

"They're good," Rory assured her.

Helen stared at him. "And Ike?" Her tone slid right from cool politeness to venomous.

With reason. Helen was no fan of Ike, and Ike felt the same way about her. She had plenty of disapproval for Dutton and him for her sister's death, but she downright hated Ike. In fact, it'd been Helen who'd talked her sister into signing over the ranch to Dutton. It had essentially cut Ike out of being a part of the ranch that he had run for several decades.

"I'm guessing Ike has a reason for being here," Helen commented. She glanced in the direction of the ER doors.

Rory heard the footsteps before he even turned to see Ike storming toward them, and judging from his expression, he was spoiling for a fight. Good. So was Rory, and he wasn't in the mood to take any flak off his father.

"Make one wrong move, and I'll arrest you," Rory snarled. He aimed his index fingers as a warning to Ike.

"One wrong move?" Ike howled, and he didn't stop until he was right in front of them. "I'd say you already did that by demanding I come in to be grilled." He spared Eden and Helen a narrow-eyed glance. "Did one of them convince you that I've done something to get me locked in a cage?"

"No, the evidence did that all on its own," Rory replied, firing right back at him. "Your ex-girlfriend, a woman you threatened right in front of me, was brutally assaulted. During the grilling, I'll expect you to give me a full, truthful account of what went on between Brenda and you."

Ike kept his glare on Rory a moment longer before he shifted to Helen. She seemed to be enjoying this moment a little too much.

"Did you try to kill your ex...again?" Helen asked. There was a taunt in her voice. "I mean, technically my sister wasn't your ex, and you didn't actually murder her, but you sure as hell contributed to her death."

Rory sighed. This certainly wasn't the first time he'd heard his aunt voice that particular theory. And she might even be right. When Rory's mom, Doreen, had been diagnosed with cancer and been told she had six months to live, Ike hadn't gotten her to receive traditional treatment, but instead had encouraged her to go to an experimental clinic in Mexico. She'd died within three weeks.

"Well?" Helen persisted. "Did you try to kill this woman, too?"

Ike took one menacing step toward his former sister-in-law. "At the moment, you're the only woman I'd like to see dead, Helen," he snarled, though he shot a glance at Eden to indicate she might be on this hit list, too.

"Enough of this," Rory snapped, and he moved between Ike and Helen. "Time for you to go home," he said to his aunt before shifting to his father. "And you need to go to the police station. I'll be there after I question Brenda."

Both Helen and Ike went silent, and Rory tried to figure out what the heck their expressions meant. Were those nerves he saw?

"Question her..." Helen murmured. "Good," she added a heartbeat later. "Maybe she'll remember everything Ike did to her."

Apparently, Helen decided that was a good thing to say before exiting, because then she turned and walked away.

Ike didn't. "What did Brenda say when you found her?" he asked.

Not spoken like a demand but rather...what? A plea? Maybe. But Rory could take that two ways. Either Ike genuinely cared about what had happened to Brenda, or else he was worried she'd rat him out. Rory didn't get the chance to find out because he saw the doctor, Amy Calvert, heading their way.

"Stay here," Rory warned Ike, and Eden and he went to the doctor so that Ike wouldn't be privy to whatever they said.

One look at Dr. Calvert's face, though, and Rory knew. Hell. He knew. That's why her words weren't a surprise. Still, they gave him a gut punch.

"I'm sorry," Dr. Calvert said, keeping her voice at a whisper. "But Brenda Watford is dead."

Chapter Three

Two unsolved murders.

That was the thought going through Eden's head as she dealt with the chaos of the morning. Unlike other kinds of chaos, though, most of this was thoroughly enjoyable.

Not the pressing worry about the murders, of course.

Not her continuing battle with the grief over losing Mellie, either.

But rather the hectic morning routine of being a mom to a nine-month-old baby. A baby who could crawl lightning-fast, babble nonstop and make a thorough mess of the blueberry oatmeal he was having for breakfast. Eden was mopping up some of that oatmeal on Tyler's face while he wiggled and tried to duck away from the washcloth.

She turned at the sound of the footsteps, already knowing who it was. Leslie and Rory. Eden had heard the nanny letting Rory inside, which meant he was right on time. He'd never missed an 8:00 a.m. visit since she and Tyler had moved back to Renegade Canyon.

"Dada Dada," Tyler squealed. He clapped his hands, flinging the oatmeal far and wide. Leslie laughed and hurried to get another wet cloth to help with the cleanup.

"Did he get any breakfast in his mouth?" Rory asked, going to Tyler and giving him a kiss on the top of his head.

Rory also ended up having to pick a fleck of oatmeal off his own lips.

"Not much," Eden muttered, looking up at Rory.

Their gazes met, and she saw what his smile couldn't hide. He hadn't slept well. With reason. They had another murder on their hands, and their prime suspect was his father.

Ike wasn't exactly cooperating, either. He'd given "no comment" to every question in their interview with him, and when his trio of lawyers had arrived, they'd insisted the interview be postponed until this morning. They'd had another demand, too. That any future questioning not be done by his son and his son's former partner.

Legally, it was a valid request since it was a conflict of interest, but that could be said of everyone in the entire police department. Ike knew every single one of them, and he didn't get along with any of them. Still, Ike didn't have a personal connection to Deputy Livvy Walsh, and since she was on the day shift, anyway, she would be the one to conduct the interview.

In the meantime, Ike hadn't been locked up because there hadn't been enough evidence to hold him. It hadn't been easy for Eden to watch him just walk out of the police station. It'd felt as if once again, she was letting Mellie down. But she'd had to remind herself that Ike might not have been Mellie's killer, and he might not have murdered Brenda, either.

"You okay?" Rory asked her, and he continued to study her. He was no doubt seeing the fatigue from the restless night she'd had.

"I'm fine," Eden said. "You?"

He nodded, and their gazes continued to hold. And there

it was. Along with the concern was the heat that neither of them wanted.

Really?

Now?

As she usually did, Eden silently cursed it and tore her attention from him. Sometimes, just looking at Rory fueled the attraction. Sometimes, it came no matter what she did or didn't do.

"I can take over if you two want to go ahead and leave," Leslie offered.

Their leaving definitely wasn't part of the morning routine. Usually, they spent several hours with Tyler in his playroom, or if the weather was good, they took him to the pasture to see the horse that Rory had given Tyler. But that routine would have to be broken today since they needed to make another trip to the crime scene. The CSIs were already there, and with some luck, they might have some info for them.

Eden nodded, stood and kissed her son. "Mama and Dada will be back," she said, purposely not adding a *soon* to that.

Because Eden had no idea how long the trip would take, and after that, she wanted to observe Ike's interview. Rory would no doubt want to do the same thing.

Rory gave their son a kiss, too, causing Tyler to beam a smile at him. That was usual as well. Tyler clearly loved his daddy, and while Eden couldn't say it was exactly comfortable having Rory around and in such close contact, she knew they were doing what was best for their son. They were putting aside their differences and co-parenting.

Coinvestigating, too.

Which meant that close contact with Rory would continue for a while.

That also meant dealing with the constant rounds of this attraction that just wouldn't go away.

Still silently cursing herself, they left the house, heading for his cruiser, which he'd parked in her driveway. "I talked to Dewey Galway on the drive to your place," he said, referring to the medical examiner, and Eden heard the dread in his voice. "He's still doing the postmortem, but he was able to tell me that the cause of Brenda's death was the blood loss from the stab wounds. There were six of them."

"Six," she muttered. "A lot."

"Yeah. Not what the ME would call a frenzy, and in fact, he thought the killer might have been trying to avoid any major organs. For instance, there were no wounds near the heart."

She gave that some thought as they stood outside the cruiser. "So the killer didn't want her dead right away. He wanted her to suffer?"

Rory shrugged. "Or the killer didn't know what he was doing." He shook his head. "It doesn't make sense. Why stab a woman six times and leave without making sure she's dead?"

Yes, that was puzzling. Unless the killer did indeed believe she was dead. Or perhaps he'd been interrupted and had had to flee. Though Eden couldn't imagine what kind of interruption would pull a murderer away from his prey when they were in such a remote location like the barn. Still, it was possible the dog had startled him or had become aggressive, causing him to run.

"Brenda had also been drugged," Rory went on. "She'd been roofied."

Eden silently groaned. Rohypnol was a fairly easy drug to obtain, and it was even easier to slip into a drink. So did that mean Brenda had been in close contact with her killer, close enough for the killer to have spiked her drink?

She continued to mull over that scenario while she told Rory about a call she'd gotten earlier from the sheriff. "Grace is champing at the bit to come back to work," she told him. "But thankfully, Dutton convinced her to stay put."

"Yeah, I talked to Dutton on the way over. The doctor won't clear Grace for duty yet."

Not a surprise, since she'd needed a C-section to deliver her son, Nash, only three weeks ago. Grace needed to recover and spend time with her newborn.

"I also got a call from SAPD this morning," Rory went on as they got in the cruiser and started the drive to the barn. "Brenda had a stalker. A guy named Carter Rooney. She had a restraining order against him."

That got Eden's attention. "An ex-boyfriend? And was there violence involved?"

"Not a boyfriend and no record of actual violence. Carter claims Brenda ruined him financially." Rory paused. "However, he has left threatening voice mails and texts for Brenda, and he doesn't have an alibi for last night. SAPD will be questioning him."

"Good." And since Eden still had plenty of contacts at SAPD, she shouldn't have any problem getting a recording and summary report of that interview. "We'll need to talk to Carter as well," she added.

"Yes. I'll set that up for later today. Depending on what comes out of his interview with SAPD, we might have to go to him."

She made a sound of agreement. There might not be enough compelling evidence to force Carter to come to

Renegade Canyon. Still, it would be worth the drive to talk to him in person.

Rory took the turn off the main road and onto the ranch trail. Where they immediately hit a huge pothole. The surface of the trail had gotten worse since their trip here the night before, no doubt from the influx of traffic. First the killer, then Rory and her, followed by the ambulance and now the CSIs.

They were still a good quarter of a mile from the barn when Rory's phone rang and Dispatch popped up on the dash screen. Rory answered it right away on speaker.

"Deputy McClennan, you have a call from a Diedre Bennington," the dispatcher said. "She wants to talk to you."

The name was vaguely familiar to Eden, but she couldn't quite recall who the woman was. Rory didn't seem to have that problem because he muttered some profanity under his breath.

"Put the call through," he instructed and glanced at her. "Diedre is another of my dad's ex-girlfriends. In fact, he was having an affair with her at the time my mother died."

Sweet heaven. Eden groaned. She had always known Ike was a jerk, but she hadn't known that he'd cheated on his dying wife.

"There's bad blood between Ike and Diedre?" she asked.

"Oh, yeah," Rory confirmed just as the woman's voice began to pour through the speakers.

"Rory," she said with a whole lot of rushed breath in just that simple greeting. "I heard about the dead woman. The second one. Both enemies of your father. Am I next?" Diedre blurted. "Is Ike coming after me?"

"There's no indication of that, Diedre," Rory commented, but there wasn't much assurance in his voice.

With good reason. Ike might be doing just that. Eliminating some old grudges.

Including the one he'd had with Mellie.

But as a cop, Eden had to look at the whole picture here. And set aside her personal hatred for Ike. A person didn't just start a killing spree unless there was some kind of trigger. She just wasn't seeing that.

Not yet, anyway.

But she made a mental note to look into Ike's finances and health. Getting bad news about those things could sometimes send a person over the edge. Also, with his seventieth birthday coming up, Ike could feel he was running out of time to settle some old scores.

"Have you arrested Ike?" Diedre asked.

"No." And Rory didn't add to that. "But if you're worried about your safety, you should take precautions. Is there a friend or relative you can stay with for a while?"

"Yes," she said on a sob. "But if you just arrest him, I'll be safe. All of his enemies will be safe. You have to know Ike's behind this. Don't let your family ties blind you to what Ike is."

Rory groaned and shook his head. If anyone was aware of the kind of man Ike was, it was Rory.

"I'll let you know if and when Ike is taken into custody," Rory told the woman. "And I have to go. If you have any immediate issues with a threat, you should contact SAPD since you're in their jurisdiction."

"But they can't arrest him," Diedre spluttered. "You can."

"Call SAPD if there's a threat," he repeated.

With that, Rory ended the call and dragged in a long, weary breath. Maybe because he hadn't wanted to deal with the woman who had possibly caused his mother some emotional pain. Of course, there could be many of Ike's ex-lovers who'd done that.

Rory immediately made a call to someone they knew. Detective Hailey Patterson at SAPD. Eden had worked with her, and he had met her several times when she and Rory had been in one of their on-again cycles.

Hailey's call went to voice mail, and Rory left a message to let the detective know about Diedre's concerns for her safety. There wasn't much SAPD could actually do in situations like this. Not even man power to provide personal security when there hadn't actually been an attempt to harm Diedre. Still, the woman would be on SAPD's radar in case something did happen.

"Even if Ike is the killer, I can't see him going after her," Eden muttered. "Not when there's this much attention focused on him." But then she stopped, and rethought that comment. "Unless he has some kind of urgency to rid the world of people on his bad side."

Rory didn't seem the least bit surprised by her last remark, which meant the same idea had likely already occurred to him. "I can't get access to his medical records, but I'll have a talk with the housekeepers and Jamie."

"Jamie," she repeated. Not a question.

She knew that was Rory's twelve-year-old cousin, who lived in the main house on the ranch with Ike and her parents. Rory had told her that because of the age difference, he'd always thought of Jamie as his niece, and they were fairly close. It was possible Jamie had seen or heard something that would shed some light on whether or not there'd been a trigger for Ike to start killing.

"Do you think you should try to encourage Jamie and her folks to stay elsewhere?" Eden asked.

"I advised them to do that this morning before I went

to your place. But Ike doesn't consider them enemies. They'd never crossed him. Never butted heads with him over something Ike wanted."

The way Ike had butted heads with Rory and her.

Good. She was glad the girl and her parents weren't having to face that kind of ugly wrath.

Eden looked up when the barn came into view and felt exactly what she'd been expecting. That overwhelming sense of dread. It didn't matter that the barn was no longer cloaked in darkness. Sunshine and a clear sky weren't going to diminish the eerie feel of the place or lessen her memories of what had gone on there.

As expected, the county CSI van was parked off the trail and in a small clearing beneath some trees, and she saw one of the CSI team, dressed in his white protective jumpsuit, boot covers and gloves. He was stooped down, looking at something on the right side of the barn, but he glanced in their direction when they got out of the cruiser. Eden figured there was at least one other CSI inside.

They made their way to the investigator outside, and as she got closer, she saw it was Lou Garcia, a fairly new CSI. But he had worked the same barn after Mellie's murder.

"Have you found anything?" Rory immediately asked him.

Lou motioned toward an even smaller trail on the far side of the barn. "We found tire tracks over there, but they were practically obliterated. Looks like some deer trampled over them. Still, I took a casting so we might come up with something."

Eden frowned when she turned toward the trail. She wished that they had looked there the night before, but it'd been too dark for them to see much of anything. Added to that, their focus had been on getting Brenda some help and talking to her to see if she could ID her attacker.

"That trail's even rougher than the one we used," Rory remarked.

"Yes, it is," Lou agreed. "If the killer came that way, he or she would have needed an off-road vehicle, and even that wouldn't have been a pleasant drive." He shifted and pointed toward the back of the barn. "There were drag marks there. Along with some of the victim's blood."

"So she was bleeding before he put her in the barn," Rory muttered. "That means whatever vehicle he used would have her blood, too. And there'd be blood at the location where she was attacked."

They were looking for another crime scene. SAPD had already ruled out Brenda's house and office, so the next step would be to search Ike's house.

Rory took out his phone and requested a warrant to have the CSIs examine all of Ike's vehicles and the main house. She was betting Ike and his lawyers would fight that, but it was a fight they'd lose. With Ike's motive and means, and with no verifiable alibi, that would be enough for a judge to issue a warrant.

Once he'd finished his call, the two of them started toward the front of the barn. "The attack happened elsewhere," he said as if spelling it all out for himself. "And the killer brought her here. Not an easy trip. And a risky one. Why take that risk?"

"To make some kind of statement," she mused. "To put her in the same place as Mellie."

Rory stopped in the entry of the barn and turned to her. "But he didn't put her in the same place. He put her at the back of the barn. And he didn't use the same trail to get here. He used one that's more visible from the main road."

True, and that caused Eden's mind to whirl with possibilities. "We didn't disclose the exact location of Mellie's body in any of the reports." She stopped, cursed. "And that means we could be dealing with a copycat."

"Bingo," he murmured, and she could see the worry in his eyes.

Two victims. Two killers. And if one of those killers wasn't his father, then someone was trying to set Ike up.

They were about to step inside when they heard the approaching vehicle. A motorcycle. They turned to see Rory's brother, Dutton, and he pulled his Harley to a stop behind the cruiser.

"A problem?" Rory immediately asked. "Is the baby all right?"

"He's fine," Dutton said, nodding a greeting to Eden. He walked closer, stopping next to them and staring at the barn. "I considered just calling you, but I decided this was a conversation best done in person."

Rory sighed. "You're here to tell me something that could get Ike arrested," he said, guessing.

"No. Not Ike," Dutton said. "Aunt Helen."

Eden didn't know who was more surprised by that, Rory or her. "What did she do?" Rory asked.

"It could be nothing, but it's been eating away at me all night." Dutton gathered his breath. "Two days ago, Helen came to the ranch. I know because I happened to be taking out one of the new horses for a ride, and I spotted her with Ike. They were on the back porch, arguing. About what, I couldn't tell, but as I rode closer, Helen whipped out a knife from her purse and seemed to threaten Ike with it."

Sweet heaven. "Neither one of them mentioned a word about this," Eden said.

"That doesn't surprise me," Dutton grumbled. "I got off

the horse and hurried to them, and when Helen looked in my direction, Ike knocked the knife from her hand. Then, he mocked her, saying she was nothing but a coward. Always had been, always would be. He continued to goad her until she burst into tears and ran off the porch. She got in her car and sped away."

Eden shook her head. "What was the argument about?"

"Ike wouldn't say. I called Aunt Helen, and she finally answered a couple of hours later. She said it was all a misunderstanding." Dutton shrugged. "Maybe it was. Ike and Helen have certainly had a lot of clashes over the years."

Rory made a sound of agreement. "But I've never known Helen to pull a knife on him. What did Ike say about the incident?"

"He laughed it off, insisted it was no big deal, that Helen had just gotten her dander up, and he added a few more clichés, like making a mountain out of a molehill."

It didn't sound like a molehill to her. "What did Ike do with the knife?" Eden asked.

Dutton shook his head. "I don't know. It wasn't on the porch by the time I got back there after I went to check on Helen." He paused. "Why? You think it was the murder weapon?"

"Well, we don't have the murder weapon so it's possible. What did the knife look like?" she persisted.

"It was one of those Swiss Army ones. Not a long blade. Maybe three inches," Dutton answered.

Rory took out his phone again. "I'm texting the ME to see if he can determine the depth of the stab wounds on Brenda's body." He finished the message and looked at his brother. "And I'll talk to Helen."

Dutton sighed. "Yeah, that'll be fun." He glanced around. "I'll leave you to it. Let me know, though, what Helen says."

"I will," Rory assured him. They said their goodbyes and as Dutton headed back to his motorcycle, she and Rory went inside the barn.

Once again, she had to force her attention away from the stain of Mellie's blood. It was easier to do that today since she could focus on the two CSIs, Molly Hanks and David Barrow, who were working all the way at the back of the barn. There was enough light coming through the cracks that she could see they were examining something on the wall.

Rory must have noticed, too, because their pace quickened. Maybe the CSIs had found something they could use.

They stopped a few feet from the stall, and Rory opened his mouth, no doubt to question them. He didn't get the chance.

Because an explosion ripped through the barn.

Chapter Four

Rory heard the deafening blast. Felt it, too, when his body jolted and then lunged forward. He couldn't stop himself from being hurled into one of the stalls, and he landed, hard, on what was left of the hay-strewn floor.

The impact knocked the breath right out of him, and while fighting for air was a high priority, he was also trying to register what had happened.

Some kind of explosion had torn through the barn.

Debris was falling all around him, and there was the sound of someone moaning. Someone in pain.

Eden.

She was hurt, and he had to get to her. But he couldn't see her. The air was a cloud of dust, filled with bits of rubble and smoke.

Hell.

Was the barn on fire? He couldn't see or feel any flames, but at the moment the only things he could feel were the vise-like pressure in his chest and the all-consuming need to get to Eden so he could help her.

Grappling for air, Rory clutched his chest, and he managed to get to his feet. There were more of those moans, but he couldn't be sure if it was Eden or one of the CSIs. Someone was definitely hurt.

He caught on to what was left of the stable wall so he could try to propel himself forward. Thankfully, nothing in his body seemed to be broken, and he was slowly regaining his breath.

With the much-needed air filling his lungs, Rory had the strength to move, and he glanced around, picking through the heaps of wood and other junk that was scattered pretty much everywhere. He certainly couldn't see Eden or the CSIs, so he moved out even farther and continued glancing around.

Most of the barn wall directly ahead of him was gone. The blast had torn a huge chunk out of it, and the gaping hole was large enough to drive a vehicle through. His stomach dropped when he realized that was the area that the CSI, Lou Garcia, had been checking when he and Eden had arrived. Rory prayed the guy was all right, but he wasn't seeing any movement outside.

No movement inside, either.

But he heard that groan again.

"Eden?" he called out.

It seemed to take an eternity for her to answer. An eternity where Rory had to battle the worst-case scenarios to keep them out of his head. He couldn't lose Eden. He just couldn't.

"Here," she finally said. Like him, her breathing was labored, but he could pinpoint her location in the stall next to him.

The stall where Brenda had been left to die.

Rory used his hand to try to wave away some of the cloudy particles that were obstructing his vision. He stepped over some of the pieces of shattered wood and inched his way to the stall.

And he saw Eden.

Alive.

The relief flooded through him. But not for long, because while Eden was on her feet and staggering toward him, the CSIs, Molly and David, were still on the floor. Molly was moaning, and there was blood on her head. But David wasn't even moving. He was either unconscious or dead.

In the back of his mind, Rory realized the crime scene had literally been blown to hell and back, and that the killer was likely responsible. But he couldn't focus on that now. He went to Eden, and before he could stop himself, he pulled her into his arms.

She didn't resist. In fact, she hugged him right back.

"Are you hurt?" he asked.

She shook her head. "I don't think so. Just dazed. You?"

"Same." He hoped. The right side of his chest was throbbing like a bad tooth, so he might not actually be injury-free after all.

Rory wanted to keep her in his arms, but he knew that couldn't happen. He eased back, managed to take out his phone and called Dispatch to request an ambulance, backup and the county bomb squad. Heaven knew how long it would take them to get out here, but Rory wanted a thorough investigation on the cause of the explosion.

First, though, he had to tend to the wounded.

Eden was obviously on the same wavelength because she went to Molly, and Rory went to David. He checked for a pulse and found one. Weak, but the man was still alive. Rory wanted him to stay that way.

There were three ragged-edged boards on David's chest, and Rory gently pushed them aside so he could check for injuries. Beside him, Eden was doing the same thing to Molly, who was bleeding from what appeared to be a gash on her forehead. That wound in itself didn't look critical, but it was possible the woman had a severe concussion.

Once he had the boards off David, Rory spotted the blood. It was seeping through the top of the CSI jumpsuit. Not a lot of it, but enough for Rory to know David had been cut or injured by the flying debris. Thankfully, he was breathing on his own, but he still wasn't conscious, and he didn't react when Rory tapped his cheek.

"Lou," Molly muttered.

Rory looked at the woman to see if she had spotted her fellow CSI, but she hadn't. Instead, she was looking at that massive hole in the barn wall.

Eden's gaze met his, and he immediately saw the concern in her eyes. Rory was concerned, too, because it was possible Lou had been right on top of the explosive device when it went off.

"I'll check on him," Rory said.

Then, he had a debate what to do. He considered telling Eden to get Molly to the cruiser. But that came with risks.

Huge ones.

Because the killer could be out there, waiting for them to come rushing out of the barn. Added to that, it probably wasn't a good idea to leave David alone. If he stopped breathing, Eden would need to try to save him by starting CPR.

"Be careful," Eden told him as he moved away from her.

"You, too." And he gave her one last look before he started across the barn.

It wasn't a fast trek to go across the thirty or so feet of space, since there were more of those chunks of wood everywhere. Some of the pieces were now sticking up like giant splinters, and if he fell on one of those, he'd have more than aching ribs.

Rory had no choice but to step on some of the debris. He wobbled a few times, regained his balance and kept moving. He tried not to think that there could be a second explosive device.

No. Best not to think of that.

While he walked, he tried to listen for any sounds to indicate the third CSI was alive. Any sounds of the killer, too, but the only thing he could hear was Eden murmuring something to Molly, and the breeze stirring the trees outside.

Rory finally made it to the hole so he could look out, and he saw yet more debris there as well. What he didn't see was the CSI. Not at first, anyway. Then, he spotted him about five yards away. Bloody and unmoving.

Hell.

Rory couldn't see any signs of life, and he started through the hole so he could hurry to him. The sound stopped him.

A sound he sure as hell hadn't wanted to hear.

It hadn't come from Eden or any of the CSIs, but rather from overhead. The barn roof creaked, and the sound soon turned into something much louder. Much worse.

The roof was caving in.

"Eden!" Rory shouted.

That was all he managed to get out before all hell broke loose. Wood and steel beams came down with a loud swoosh, crashing onto the floor and creating another of those clouds of debris.

"Eden," he called out again.

He couldn't see her. Couldn't hear her. If she was saying anything or even moving, the sound was muffled by more of the roof falling. From the sound of it, every board and beam of it was coming down, and Eden and the two CSIs would be trapped.

Rory had to rein in the overwhelming urge to run to her. To try to cover Eden with his body and protect her. But he'd never make it to her. With all the wood and steel falling, he'd be crushed.

Or killed.

The roof surface and the support beams were slamming onto the ground, causing the sides of the barn to start shaking. Mercy. What was left of the walls could collapse on them as well.

He had to risk it. He had to get to Eden so he could try to get the CSIs and her to safety. Muttering a prayer, Rory took off, dodging the chunks and sheets of wood raining down around him.

When he was about ten feet away from the place where he'd last seen Eden, Rory finally spotted her. Eden and Molly were trying to get David through a large hole of the barn. They were struggling since they, too, were having to avoid getting hit by the falling debris. Added to that, David was still unconscious, so it would have been like moving dead weight.

Rory continued to move, keeping his attention fixed on Eden, and he was close enough for their gazes to meet when another chunk of the roof came down. He could do nothing to stop it. Rory could only watch as it fell, slamming down right on Eden and the CSIs.

The emotions tore through him. *Get to her now. Save her.* And he got the motherlode of adrenaline to fuel him forward. Rory figured the roof would continue to fall. Hell, the whole place would, and he might get hit, but for now, his focus was on getting to Eden.

Feeding off that adrenaline, Rory tore his way through the wood, trying to avoid the rusty nails sticking out from some of the pieces. He just kept tossing aside what he could until he saw something.

The lower half of a body.

It took him a second to realize it wasn't Eden. It was David, and while Eden and Molly had apparently managed to get him partially through the hole, they hadn't gotten him fully through.

And his legs had been crushed by one of the support beams.

Rory had no idea if the man was still alive, and he couldn't take the time to find out. Not when yet more of the roof slammed down directly behind him. Every second counted now, if he hoped to get out of this alive, so he flipped the beams over and pushed them aside. Normally, that would have been a much harder task, but it was obvious the wood was rotting.

The moment Rory had David free, he took hold of him and pushed him through the opening. He had some help because Eden and Molly were right there, and they grabbed on to David, sliding him the rest of the way out.

Rory followed him.

The moment he was outside, he lifted David into a fireman's carry, tossing him over his shoulder. Rory prayed that wasn't making the man's injuries even worse, but he had no choice. He had to get them away from here.

"Move," Rory told Eden and Molly.

They did. They turned and started running. Rory was right behind them, and not a second too soon.

The entire barn crashed to the ground.

Chapter Five

Eden winced as the nurse cleaned a small cut on her forehead. It was the fourth one, and there were still several more to go. Thankfully, none of them were serious. In fact, Eden could have tended them at home, but Rory had insisted she be examined after their ordeal at the barn.

Where they could have been killed.

Eden couldn't push that thought aside. Couldn't push away the memories of seeing the roof fall while Rory was still in the center of the barn. It was a miracle he hadn't been crushed when the roof caved in.

Lou hadn't been so lucky. He was dead, killed instantly by whatever explosive had been set off just outside the barn. Eden didn't have an official report on it yet, but she suspected Lou had been right by, or even on, the device. The young man hadn't stood a chance of surviving.

David hadn't come out of the ordeal unscathed, either. He was in surgery for internal injuries he'd sustained from the falling support beam. She did have an official report on him that'd come from one of the doctors. David was critical but was expected to live.

Like Rory and her, Molly's injuries were mostly superficial. Cuts, scrapes and bruises. Molly had been admitted to the hospital, though, for an overnight stay because of the hit she'd taken to the head. The doctors didn't think it was serious, but they wanted to keep an eye on her.

And speaking of keeping an eye on someone, that's exactly what Rory was doing to her.

He was sitting in the chair in the treatment room, talking on his phone and watching as her injuries were treated. He'd already gone through the process and was now sporting a butterfly bandage on his forehead and three Band-Aids on his left arm.

Eden knew this particular call Rory was making was to the nanny, to check on Tyler. But before that, there'd been one to Grace to update her. Then, several to the on-duty deputies. He hadn't put any of the calls on speaker, probably because medical staff were coming and going from the treatment room, but he'd managed to give her updates on the investigation when they'd gotten a moment or two to themselves.

Deputy Livvy Walsh was the senior officer in the squad room, so she was coordinating things with the bomb squad and the CSIs who'd been called in from another county. The explosion had put their own county's team out of commission, and the scene at the barn would have to be processed.

Eden wasn't holding out much hope the CSIs would find something to help them with Brenda's murder. The explosion would have likely destroyed any potential evidence. And that was no doubt the reason it'd been set.

By the killer.

It ate away at her to think the killer could have been there. Right there, where she and Rory could have caught him. Now more than ever she wanted this monster behind bars. And she wanted to know if he or she had also killed

Mellie. That was a wound that wouldn't even start to heal until she'd gotten the woman the justice she deserved.

"What did Leslie say?" Eden asked him the moment he finished his call with the nanny.

"Tyler's fine," he assured her. "He's napping right now, but Leslie's going to take him outside to see the horse when he's awake."

Good. That was the routine that Eden and Rory had with Tyler, and Eden hadn't wanted him to miss out on one of his favorite activities. She wished she could be there, to see the enjoyment she knew Tyler would get from it, but they needed to stick with this investigation.

Because they had a possible serial killer on their hands.

Mellie, Brenda and now Lou. That was the magic number for the gut-twisting label of serial killer. And it was even harder to accept since it could be Rory's own father.

Or his aunt.

Eden certainly wasn't forgetting what Dutton had told them about Helen. It was hard for her to imagine Helen being enraged enough to kill and frame Ike, but she couldn't rule out that possibility. So, yes, she and Rory needed to press hard on this investigation, to put an end to the body count.

Rory stood and went closer, checking out the cut on her head as the nurse, Beatrice Garcia, put on the last of the bandages. Eden had known Beatrice for years, and the woman gave Eden a pat on the hand before she picked up her supplies.

"Wait here, and I'll get some paperwork you'll need to sign," Beatrice said. "Both of you," she added to Rory as she exited the area.

Rory moved even closer, leaning down and pulling her into a gentle hug. It wasn't exactly a professional response, but it was a welcome one. She needed him for just a moment so she could steady herself.

The hug didn't last long, and when Rory eased back from her, their gazes met. He said a single word of profanity. Then, he groaned.

She knew what that reaction was about. It was about the entire mess that was now their lives. They were in this together, and somehow they had to ID the killer and stop them.

"Ike's interview has been delayed," he said, checking his watch. "We've got about an hour. You think you're up to it, or would you rather just head home—"

"I'm up to it," Eden said, not able to say the words fast enough. "No way do I want to miss that."

Even though Rory and her wouldn't be the ones doling out the questions. Still, they'd be able to hear what the man had to say.

Rory nodded as if that'd been the exact answer he'd expected from her. "Ike's lawyers have told Livvy that he was with them during the time of the explosions," he went on. "So an alibi for that."

She shook her head. "That doesn't mean anything, right? The bomb could have been set before we even arrived at the barn or maybe even the night before, when Brenda was left there."

"Yes," he agreed. "That was in the preliminary report from the bomb squad." Rory glanced at his phone. "I got a text update from them while you were getting bandaged, and they said it was basically an IED that had likely been placed in a shallow hole. When Lou stepped on it, it went off."

Eden suppressed a shudder. Barely. That IED had cost a man his life, but it could have killed all of them had they been on that side of the barn.

Rory pulled up a photo. "The bomb guys believe the IED looked something like this."

She studied the tan-colored PCV pipe that had likely contained the explosive material. Along with that, there was wiring, a small battery and some kind of switch that she supposed was the detonator. It seemed small enough for a half dozen or more to fit into a backpack.

"What kind of expertise would it take to make something like that?" Eden asked, because she was having trouble picturing Ike putting together this dangerous device and then transporting it to the barn.

"Sadly, not much," Rory explained. "Instructions for that kind of stuff can be found on the internet. The bomb squad will gather all the parts of the IED and examine it." He paused. "It's possible that it wasn't homemade, that it was done by a pro."

Now, she could see Ike doing something like that. Despite not being the actual owner of the McClennan family ranch, the man still had money. Eden had learned that during the time she'd investigated him as a person of interest in Mellie's murder. When Ike and his wife had married, he'd sold his own ranch for nearly a million before moving to his wife's family place, and Ike had made some good investments with the cash from that sale. Added to that, Ike and his younger brother had split a ten-million-dollar estate when their parents had passed away.

So the bottom line was that Ike could afford the best. And if that's what he had done, then the best IED maker might be hard to catch since he or she would likely know how to cover their tracks. Still, the bomb squad might find something that would help them unravel this.

"I also got another call from Diedre," Rory continued a moment later. He was staying close to her, close enough that his left side was against her leg, and he had lowered his voice. No doubt so that no one passing by the treatment room would overhear them. "She offered to set herself up as bait for Ike to come after her."

Of all the things Eden had been expecting him to say, that wasn't one of them. "Bait? Last night she was terrified that Ike was going to kill her."

He nodded, and his expression conveyed his mixed feelings about that. "She could have been exaggerating. And if she was, then I have to speculate as to why. Did she think she could convince us to arrest Ike? Maybe," he concluded. "Or she could have just wanted to plant that seed in our minds."

"The seed was already there," Eden pointed out.

"Yeah, it was, but Diedre might have wanted to try to speed things up. She could be doing that with this bait idea, too."

Eden gave that some thought. And she saw how this could play out. "Diedre allows herself to be in a position where Ike could come after her, and then she somehow arranges for Ike to be there, too, before the cops run in to rescue her."

"That's what I figure she had in mind, as well. She could have even planned to goad Ike into attacking her so that it would add to the evidence against him." He looked her straight in the eyes. "I declined Diedre's offer."

Yes. Eden had known he would. Because for one thing it was dangerous. If Ike truly was the killer, he could murder Diedre before the cops could stop him. And if he was innocent and did little or nothing to the woman, Ike's lawyers could add that it was entrapment. Either way, a bait situation like that wouldn't end well for anyone.

"So is Diedre a suspect in the murders?" Eden asked.

Rory opened his mouth but didn't get a chance to answer because his phone rang. When he took it from his pocket, she saw Livvy's name on the screen and knew he had to take it right away.

"You're on speaker," he said after issuing a greeting. "Eden is here with me, and she's listening in."

"Good," Livvy said. "It'll save you from having to update her. Ike is here with his lawyers," she went on after gathering her breath. "I've put them in the interview room, but I'll wait until Eden and you are here before I start. Any idea when that'll be?"

"I'm guessing about fifteen or twenty minutes. We're just waiting on some paperwork."

"No rush," Livvy told him. "It might do Ike some good to stew a while. The more riled he is, the more likely he is to blurt something out."

"I agree," Rory and Eden said in unison.

"And besides, there's something we need to go over before the interview," Livvy continued. "I just got Brenda's phone records, and it includes copies of her texts for the past month."

That was routine in a criminal investigation, so Eden figured Livvy must have found something. Hopefully, something that would help them confirm who'd killed the woman.

"In the past two weeks Brenda sent a half-dozen texts to a number that the techs have identified as a pay-as-you-go, a burner," Livvy explained. She paused a heartbeat. "The messages are about Ike."

She felt Rory go stiff. "Read them to us," he insisted.

"All right. The first was sent exactly two weeks ago, and it seems to be a reply—'Yes, I believe Ike is behind Mellie's death.' There's no text or call from the unknown number or anyone else to tell us why Brenda sent that, but within five minutes, the unknown caller responds 'You bet your life he is.'"

So this would have been someone who knew Ike. And that led them back to Helen, or maybe Diedre.

"There's no name associated with the phone, and the phone is no longer in use," Livvy added.

That sent up a huge red flag for Eden. It must have for Rory, too, because he asked, "Any idea when the phone was discontinued?"

"I can narrow it down. Brenda sent a text to the number at three p.m. yesterday. According to the ME, that would have likely been only a couple of hours before she was attacked and left for dead. This morning when the techs tried the number, it was out of service."

So that could fit with…what? Eden had to mentally shake her head. Had this caller been connected to the killer? Or was the caller the actual killer?

"What do the rest of the texts say?" Rory asked.

"Text two again seems to be a reply with no corresponding text or phone call so it's possible it was in response to another conversation," Livvy explained. "It says 'Ike is cleaning house, and I believe you're right. He'll come after me.'"

Eden wished the woman had taken this to the cops, and they could have tried to protect her. And they might now have Mellie's killer in custody.

"The third text isn't until a week later, and it's a doozie," Livvy went on. "It says 'We need to find out who else is on Ike's hit list. Any ideas how we can do that?' The response came less than a minute later. 'I think I know someone who can bug his office and hack into his computer. Not sure he'd be careless enough to write something down, though.'"

Eden groaned. This had certainly escalated. "Was the listening device put in place?" she asked Livvy.

"Yes, according to the next text. That came two days later from the unknown number. 'Bugs have been planted in his office, truck and bedroom, and I'm listening. Will keep you posted.' To that, Brenda sent a response of 'Please do.'"

Eden met Rory's gaze, and she could see that all of this was as much of a surprise to him as it was to her.

"Request a warrant to have all three of those locations checked for listening devices," Rory stated.

"Already done. If the CSIs find them, they'll be brought in for testing. We might get prints off them. If they exist," Livvy concluded.

Yes, and that was an *if* they had to consider. Because if the unknown texter was the killer, or Ike, then all of this could be some kind of sick game the killer was playing with Brenda. There could be no listening devices.

"The fifth text also came the day Brenda was murdered," Livvy continued. "And the sender had this to say—'Overheard exactly what we suspected. Ike's cleaning house, and he named names in a meeting with a bomb expert he plans on using. Brenda, you're on the list.'"

"Hell," Rory snarled. "And what did Brenda say to that?"

"'Not surprised,'" Livvy said, continuing to read. "'Ike hates my guts. I'll be ready for him if he comes after me the way he did poor Mellie.'"

Eden felt as if someone had punched her. She'd always known Ike was a suspect, but it was a different thing to hear it all spelled out like this. Then again, the spelling out might be all lies.

"Several minutes later, Brenda sent the sixth text," Livvy continued. "And she asks 'Who else is Ike after?'"

Eden pulled in her breath, held it. Waited.

"'Me, of course,' the person texted back. 'Frank Mott, too.'"

That name was very familiar to Eden since he'd been questioned in Mellie's murder. There'd been no evidence against him, but like Ike, Frank wasn't in favor of Mellie running a foster home so close to his own ranch. He had spent years trying to get the place shut down.

But Frank also had an ongoing feud with Ike.

Eden knew that stemmed from rumors that Ike had had an affair with Frank's late wife, Miranda. There was zero evidence to support that, but Frank, like Helen, had always been vocal about Ike's cheating, and how that cheating had crushed Rory's mom, Doreen.

"There's another part to that sixth text," Livvy said, sighing. "Here it is verbatim. 'And because he wants to nip Mellie's murder investigation in the bud, Ike will be going after his son, Rory, and Deputy Eden Gallagher.'"

Chapter Six

Rory didn't know who the hell who had sent those texts to Brenda. And he couldn't even be sure they were true. But he still made the call to Sheriff Grace Granger.

"Tyler," Eden said, her breathing suddenly way too fast, and he saw the alarm all over his face.

Rory was sure he was showing some alarm, too. Not because Ike might be coming after Eden and him, but because their son might get caught in the crossfire.

Thankfully, Grace answered on the second ring, and while he hated to bother her on maternity leave, this was important.

"What's wrong?" Grace immediately asked.

"It's possible Eden and I are Ike's targets," Rory said. "Livvy has transcripts of Brenda's texts that she'll be sending you so you can see what I mean. This might be overkill, but I need Tyler protected. I'm thinking his nanny can bring him to stay with Dutton and you—"

"Absolutely," Grace interrupted. "Dutton and several of the ranch hands can go out to Eden's place and get them now."

Rory glanced at Eden to see if she was all right with that, and she gave him a quick nod while she was typing a text. No doubt to Leslie to let her know what was going on.

"Don't worry," Grace assured him. "Ike won't get near Tyler, and I'll have Dutton post some ranch hands around the house to keep guard."

That eased some of the worry inside him. Then, he cursed the fact that the threat was even a possibility. Eden and he were cops and had signed on for dangerous situations like these, but the danger shouldn't extend to their baby.

"Eden and you are welcome to stay here, too, for as long as you need," Grace went on. "How valid is the threat from Ike?"

"We don't know yet," he admitted. "We're about to leave the hospital and observe Ike's interview. He's lawyered up to his eyeballs, but if he's guilty, Livvy might be able to coax it out of him."

Grace paused. "You really think Ike's behind these murders? I want your gut feel, not only the circumstantial evidence against him."

Hell. That wasn't an easy question, but Rory did as she'd suggested and went with his gut. "I believe someone could be setting Ike up. And, no, I'm not saying that because he's my father. I'm saying it because if Ike wanted to eliminate his enemies, I doubt he'd choose to go about it this way."

Eden muttered an agreement. "Ike would have hidden the bodies better. He probably would have made the deaths seem like a botched robbery or suicide. Right now, everything points to him, and if he'd planned the murders, he should have had the evidence leading us to someone else."

"Yes, all of that makes sense. But I'll play devil's advocate. What if Ike intentionally made it seem as if he'd been set up? After all, even with a botched robbery and a suicide, he would have come under suspicion because of his bad blood with the victims. Ike could be playing a cat-

and-mouse game with the belief that if he is charged with anything, his lawyers can get him off."

Rory couldn't dispute a single word of that. Which was why Ike was still their top suspect.

"Even if Ike isn't the killer, the threat to Tyler is still there," Rory continued. "Because the person who responded to Brenda's text could be the killer. Along with setting up Ike, this person might indeed come after Eden and me."

"Yes," Grace confirmed. "And that's why the two of you will take precautions. FYI, Dutton heard what you said, and he's already heading to Eden's with the ranch hands. When Tyler and Leslie are safely here, I'll text and let you know. I'll also be watching Ike's interview through a live feed."

Good. The more eyes and ears on that interview, the better. If Ike was indeed trying to outsmart them with this sick plan, then he might give away a clue or two in something he said.

"Who else was named in those texts?" Grace asked.

"Frank Mott," Rory said. "And, of course, the person replying to Brenda's texts. No ID yet on who that is."

Grace stayed quiet a moment. "You want me to contact Frank and give him a heads-up?"

"I'll do that," Eden offered, probably to limit Grace's duties since she was on maternity leave. "And I'll ask him to come in for an interview."

"Good." Grace ended the call with a final "Be careful," and Rory stared at his phone a moment, hoping he'd done enough to protect Tyler.

Beside him, Eden located Frank's number, but the call went straight to voice mail. She left a message for the man to contact her ASAP.

As Eden put her phone away, Rory looked at her, ready to try to reassure her that their son would be all right, that he would be safe with Dutton and Grace. Before he could say anything, though, Eden reached out and pulled him into her arms.

"God, Rory. We can't let the killer get to Tyler," she muttered.

"We won't," he promised.

It was probably a mistake, but he slid his arms around her as well and eased her even closer to him. Touching Eden was always risky. Because of the blasted heat between them. Because that heat could muddle his thoughts and cause him to lose focus. But in this case, it only helped him focus even more.

They had so much at risk.

But they were a united force in protecting their child. Even with the heat, they wouldn't lose sight of that.

Rory stepped away from her when Beatrice came back in the room. The nurse gave them a long glance and seemed to be on the verge of asking them if she was interrupting. Rory nipped that in the bud. He definitely didn't want to discuss anything going on between them.

"You have the paperwork for us to sign?" he asked.

Beatrice nodded, produced some forms and two pens. Eden and he glanced over them, signed and headed out. Because of that threat looming over them, they kept watch as they went to the cruiser, got inside and pulled out.

Rory hadn't even made it out of the parking lot, though, when his phone rang, and he saw the unfamiliar number on the screen. Still, with all the moving parts of the investigation, he figured he'd be getting lots of calls from people not in his contacts.

"Deputy McClennan," the person said when Rory answered. "I'm Rachel Sanchez from Caldwell County CSI. I'm heading up the team that's been searching the residence of Ike McClennan."

Rory felt his chest tighten. "Did you find something?"

"We did. Three listening devices."

So it was true. "Where?" Rory queried.

"Two in his office and another in his bedroom. Do you know if Mr. McClennan planted the bugs himself?" Sanchez asked.

"No idea. Were they well hidden?" Rory continued.

"Two were. One was on a bookshelf. It was attached to the spine of a book. Once we found that one, we looked for others and did a thorough sweep of the house. We'll send them to the lab so they can be checked for prints or trace. They might be able to tell who was receiving the info from them."

That would be very useful information. Ditto for the prints, especially if they belonged to Ike.

"The lab will contact you if they find anything," the CSI added.

Rory hung up. And cursed.

"Yes," Eden muttered, and she expressed what had caused this latest round of frustration. "Ike will use this to say he was set up."

"He will," Rory confirmed.

And, heck, it was possible he had been.

The killer could have used the info gained from the bugs to determine where Ike would be, to ensure he didn't have solid alibis for the murders.

"Who would have had the opportunity to plant bugs?" Eden asked.

"Too many people," Rory replied. "All the cleaning staff

and the cook have the entry codes. And just last week, Asher and Kitty had a group of friends over."

That meant getting that list of friends, along with any maintenance or repair people who'd been in the house... Rory stopped, groaned. Because the bugs could have been there for months. Whover had planned these murders could have started the process ages ago.

Even though Rory was nearly at the police station, he went ahead and called Livvy to let her know about the listening devices. She would have to bring them up during the interview if for no other reason than to get Ike's take on them. He might be able to pinpoint who could have planted them.

While gloating that the bugs "proved" his innocence.

Yeah, that's exactly how it would play out.

With that thought and this whole dangerous mess weighing down on him, Rory parked and, still keeping watch, they went inside the station.

Straight into the buzz of activity.

All of the day deputies were present, each of them on the phone. Their conversations clashed with the sounds of the printer spewing out pages and yet more phones ringing. In the middle of that bustle, the black cat came sauntering toward Eden.

Sherlock was the unofficial adopted mascot who only doled out attention to a handful of people. And Eden was one of them. The cat rubbed against her legs, and Eden leaned down to give him a scratch on the head. Apparently, that was all Sherlock intended to tolerate because he turned and headed in the direction of the breakroom, where his litterbox and food dish were located.

Rory glanced in Grace's office and saw Livvy. Not alone but with someone he recognized.

Frank Mott.

The man was in his midfifties with salt-and-pepper hair, but he still sported the build of a wrestler that had apparently won him some state competitions. Photos of him were displayed in the gym at the high school.

Rory was glad the man was here so they wouldn't have to track him down. Good. They could alert him that he might be in danger.

When Livvy looked at them, Frank followed her gaze, and then he immediately started in their direction. "I just listened to your voice mail," he said, directing the comment at Eden. "I was just up the street at the hardware store and came right down."

Eden nodded, and she motioned for Frank to go back in the office. They followed, and Rory shut the door.

"Something has come to our attention," Rory began, "and it's possible you could be in danger."

Rory didn't add more. He just waited for Frank to let that sink in. Of course, it didn't sink in well.

"In danger from Ike," Frank muttered. Not in a tone of someone lashing out in anger but rather as if this was the exact news he expected to hear.

"We're not sure of that yet," Rory said, settling for caution.

Frank sighed. "It's Ike. You know it is."

Rory wished he did know for certain. But for now, he had to look at all potential suspects.

And that included Frank.

Like Helen and Diedre, there was no love lost between Ike and him, and that was the reason Rory had to ask Frank a few questions.

"Have you visited Ike at his home in the past couple of months?" he asked, figuring he already knew the answer.

"No." Yep, that was the answer Rory had expected all right, and there was still no anger in the man's voice or expression. "I haven't been to your family's ranch in years. Why? Ike didn't say I had, did he?"

Rory shook his head. "It's just a routine question." So was the next one, but Frank wasn't going to care much for it. "Where were you late yesterday afternoon and last night?"

Frank sighed again. "You want to know if I have an alibi for that woman's murder," he stated. "I don't. I was home alone, and before you ask, no one can verify that." He paused. "Don't you think if I was killing women as a vendetta against Ike, that I would have gone after his friends instead? I sure as hell wouldn't eliminate people who feel like I do about Ike."

Maybe. But murdering his friends wouldn't accomplish one important thing—setting Ike up.

"Have there been any recent altercations or arguments between the two of you?" Rory asked.

Frank laughed but not from humor. It was all sarcasm. "Ike is always getting in my face about something. As you well know, Ike and I are both on the town council, and we disagree on pretty much everything on the agenda. Last month, it was the rezoning of that land just to the east of your family's ranch. I didn't want it classified as farmland, and Ike did."

Rory knew about that. It was land Ike was trying to buy since he'd decided to get back in the ranching business. But Ike didn't want just that one section of land, he wanted Frank's place, too.

And the foster ranch that Mellie had run.

Because if Ike had all of that, the acreage would essentially coil around the McClennan family ranch, and Ike would control some of the water supply that Dutton needed for the livestock. Rory wasn't certain Ike would actually cut off that supply, but knowing Ike, it was a card he might play if the rotten mood suited him.

"Any other disputes?" Rory persisted.

Frank shrugged. "A couple of months ago, Ike undercut me on a horse I was trying to buy." Then, he paused. "And there was an, uh, incident at my wife's grave."

Rory knew about that as well. Frank's wife, Miranda, had died in a car accident about two decades ago when she was in her thirties. From all accounts, Frank had been deeply in love with her, but Miranda had cheated on him.

With Ike.

And about six months ago, a fistfight had broken out between Frank and Ike at the cemetery where Miranda was buried. Neither man had fessed up to what the altercation had been about, and no charges had been filed. The only reason Rory was even aware of it was because someone had seen the fight and reported it.

"Look, Ike and I have been at odds for years," Frank added a moment later. "I don't have the time or breath to detail every run-in I've had with him. And if I'd wanted to start killing because of him, that killing would have started twenty years ago."

When his wife had died.

Yeah, Rory could see that. But sometimes people just snapped. Sometimes, all the little things build up into something huge.

That could have happened with Frank.

"One more thing," Rory went on, aware that the time was ticking down for Ike's interview to start. "When was the last time you were at the barn on the old Sanderson Ranch?"

Frank didn't react with anger, but rather resignation and maybe some frustration at being dragged into this. It was possible the frustration was warranted, but Rory still had to treat him like a person of interest.

"Aka, the Devil's Hideout," he said, using the nickname it'd been given. "Again, the answer is years ago. You're asking because I worked there a couple of summers when I was a teenager."

Rory did indeed recall that fact from the background check that had been run on Frank after Mellie's murder.

"Mellie worked there, too, mucking stalls and grooming the palominos," Frank added. "Hell, so did a lot of teenagers. And your aunt Helen used to come out there and ride the horses sometimes."

Now, Rory didn't remember that coming up in previous interviews. He shook his head. "Why would Helen have gone there to ride when she lived on a ranch with dozens of horses?"

Frank shifted uncomfortably, and he dodged Rory's gaze for a couple of seconds. "You'd have to ask Helen about that."

"I will. But I'm also asking you," Rory retorted.

"All right." Frank dragged in a long breath. "I believe Helen was there to see me."

"See you?" Eden repeated. "As in romantically?"

Rory heard the surprise in Eden's voice, and he thought he knew why. Helen had always had that to-the-manor-born vibe about her, and Frank had come from a blue-collar family. Yes, he'd earned enough to buy his own ranch and it was successful, but in those days, Frank wouldn't have been in Helen's economic circle.

"And did Helen and you see each other?" Eden asked.

"No, we did not because I was with someone else at the

time," he insisted, and Frank looked Rory straight in the eyes. "I didn't kill those women," he repeated. "Ike did, and I hope you can do the right thing and arrest him. If not, there'll likely be another murder soon."

The man's gaze slid to Eden, and he didn't come out and say that he considered her a potential victim. While Frank's gaze wasn't accompanied with any intense emotion, it still felt like an unspoken threat.

"I'll watch my back," Frank added a moment later. "I hope everyone on Ike's bad side will do the same. Are we done here?" he asked.

"For now," Rory replied. "If I have any other questions, I'll be in touch."

Frank tipped his head in farewell, slipped on the white Stetson he'd been holding in front of him like a shield and walked out. Rory's and Eden's phones dinged with texts as they watched the man go, and Rory saw Grace's group message to both Eden and him on the screen.

Tyler and Leslie arrived at the ranch, Grace had texted. All is well. We'll keep them safe.

That helped ease some of the tension in his muscles, and he could see it had the same reaction for Eden. Tyler was their top priority, and with him safe, they could focus on their jobs.

Livvy got to her feet and began gathering her files. "Ready to start with Ike?"

Rory nodded, and he hoped the interview went a lot better than he was anticipating. It was possible as soon as those bugs were brought up that the lawyers would try to put a halt to the process by claiming it was something they needed to learn more about.

He and Eden followed Livvy down the hall, but then they peeled off, going into the observation area while

Livvy continued into the interview room. Rory immediately spotted Ike seated at the metal table, and he had two lawyers on each side of him.

Yeah, lawyered up to his eyeballs was right.

Livvy turned on the recording, adding the pertinent details of the date, time and the names of those present. She was in the process of repeating Ike's Miranda rights when Rory's phone rang.

"It's Detective Vernon from SAPD," he said to Eden.

No need for him to clarify who that was. He was the cop assigned to supervise the search of Brenda's house and office in San Antonio.

"Deputy McClennan," Rory said when he answered, "and you're on speaker with Deputy Eden Gallagher."

"Good. Because you'll both want to hear what turned up in Brenda's bedroom."

Rory silently groaned at the detective's tone, and he steeled himself for what he was certain was going to be bad news.

"The CSIs found a burner phone in a plastic bag," Vernon explained. "It was tucked away at the back of the top shelf. So, hidden from sight."

Rory's mind began to whirl with possibilities. And they weren't good possibilities, either. Some people did keep burners around for emergencies, but they didn't usually bother to hide them.

"The burner wasn't locked," the detective continued, "and there were some texts on it." He paused. "They match the replies on the messages on Brenda's other phone."

Hell in a handbasket.

"You understand what I'm saying, right?" Vernon asked.

"Oh, yeah." Rory understood all right. If the burner belonged to Brenda, then she had likely sent those texts to herself, and there was only one reason she would have done that.

To set Ike up.

"Are there any other messages on the burner, or was it used to make calls?" Rory queried.

"No. That was it, just those replies."

So the odds were Brenda had indeed planned on using those texts to try to frame Ike. Had the woman also murdered Mellie?

Maybe.

It was definitely something that needed to be investigated. In fact, it changed everything about how they needed to approach this case. And it left Rory with a huge question.

If Brenda had murdered Mellie, then who the hell had killed Brenda?

Chapter Seven

Eden was silently cursing right along with the profanity Rory was muttering. This wasn't just a setback to the case they were building against Ike, it could be the kiss the death.

She snapped back toward the observation window when she heard a phone ring. Not Rory's, but one of Ike's lawyers, Stephen Arnette. Livvy hadn't yet gotten started with the questions, but the lawyer took one look at his phone and stood.

"I need to take this," Arnette insisted. "So hold off on the interview until I get back." With that, he stepped out of the room.

It was tempting to try to listen in on the conversation, but Eden didn't want to do anything that Ike's lawyers could legally use against them, and Arnette could argue the call fell under the umbrella of client-attorney privilege. Instead, Rory used the time to text Livvy and let her know what was going on.

And, of course, Livvy's reaction wasn't good.

She tipped her eyes to the ceiling for a moment, and Eden figured she was doing some silent cursing as well.

It didn't take long—less than two minutes—before the lawyer came back in the room. Arnette certainly hadn't bothered to plaster on a poker face, and unlike Livvy, he was practically gloating.

He sank back down into his chair, and the other lawyers and Ike huddled around Arnette while they had a brief, whispered conversation before he turned his attention back to Livvy.

"I demand my client's immediate release," Arnette said. "I've just learned information that proves his innocence."

Sweet heaven. Did Arnette know about the burner phone or the bugs? Or maybe he knew about both? If so, there was a serious leak at either SAPD or among the CSIs.

"Really?" Livvy asked in a discussing-the-weather tone. "And what info would that be?"

"Unless you're completely out of touch with this investigation, Deputy," Arnette stated, "then you're aware that someone planted three listening devices in his home." His tone was both scolding and condescending. "Clearly, the real killer did that to obtain knowledge of my client's whereabouts so he could then be set up to take the blame for those poor murdered women."

"Uh-huh," Livvy countered, managing some condescension of her own. "And how exactly did you come by this information?"

Arnette didn't quite smile, but it was close enough. "I got it through an anonymous tip."

"So you have no idea if the tip is true," Livvy retorted.

That wiped some of the smugness off Arnette's face. "It is. I have confirmation from someone I trust. And, no, I'm not required to give you that name."

There were some situations in which a lawyer could be compelled to do just that as long as it didn't violate the attorney-client privilege, but this wasn't a fight worth taking on. The cat was out of the bag, and they'd have to deal with it. That, and the burner phone that'd been found at Brenda's house. That phone implied she had been the one to create Ike's hit list of enemies.

Implied.

But Eden also knew it could have been planted. Perhaps by the same person who'd planted those listening devices at Ike's.

"You have no actual proof that I killed those women," Ike stated, leaning forward and looking Livvy straight in the eyes. "Because I didn't do it. Someone is playing you, Deputy Walsh." He fanned his hand around. "Playing you and the whole damn police force, and whoever it is, they're making you all look like fools."

Eden wished she could say for sure that wasn't happening, but there were certainly a lot of pieces that didn't fit.

"Is my client free to go?" Arnette snapped.

"Not quite yet. Just a few more questions." Livvy managed a relaxed pose despite this interview having been derailed. "When was the last time you were in Brenda Watford's house?"

"Eight months ago," Ike said without hesitation.

"Wow, you seem so sure," she commented, and she didn't wait for him or his lawyers to respond. "So if we study the traffic-cam feed in and around Brenda's office, we won't see you."

Ike pulled back his shoulders. "I might be on them. I often go to San Antonio to visit friends and to eat out."

"Were any of those friends or restaurants near Brenda's house?" she continued.

"I don't think so." Ike's eyes narrowed. "Why are you asking that?"

"Because it's possible something was planted inside her house." Livvy slid a look at Arnette. "Guess your anonymous tipster didn't come through on that one for you. Or that person you rely on to confirm things." She shook her head, shifted her attention back to Ike. "Shoddy work on your lawyers' part. As much as you're paying this crew, you'd think they would be more on top of things."

Arnette muttered something under his breath that Eden didn't catch, but she figured he'd just cursed. He stood and went back into the hall, no doubt to make a call to find out what Livvy was talking about.

"Stephen Arnette exiting the interview," Livvy said for the benefit of the recording, and she shifted back to Ike. "What about your ex-lover, Diedre Bennington? When's the last time you've been to her place?"

"Months," Ike snapped. "Why? Did she lie and say I'd been there? Is she the one feeding you lies about me being a killer?"

Livvy shrugged. "She's indicated she might have some concerns about her safety when it comes to you."

Ike laughed, but there was no humor in it. "She's a liar. Hell hath no fury like a woman scorned."

"You scorned her?" Livvy asked.

Ike's mouth went tight. "I ended a relationship with her that I should have never started."

Livvy jumped right on that. "Because you were married at the time. And your wife was dying. Yes, probably not a good idea to spend time with your mistress rather than be by your wife's bedside."

Oh, Ike didn't care for that being thrown in his face. And she heard the slight shift in Rory's breathing. It had touched a nerve for him, too.

"Yeah," Ike growled. "And being with her was a mistake."

It was indeed, and that affair had been the final straw

for Rory. Before that, he'd more or less tolerated his dad. But afterward, all civility was gone between them.

Ike shook his head in disgust. "Trust me," he went on, "I've paid over and over for that mistake. Diedre has hounded me for nearly a year, trying to make my life miserable, and she turned my wife's sister against me." He jabbed his index finger at Livvy. "Those are the two you should be questioning right now. Diedre and Helen. You can bet your bottom dollar they'd recently visited Brenda."

"Why?" Livvy ventured. "Did they form an I-hate-Ike's-guts club?"

"Something like that," Ike grumbled. "I saw the three of them together in a restaurant in San Antonio."

"When was that?" Livvy persisted.

Ike lifted his shoulder. "A couple of months back. Since you're so hell-bent, why don't you check traffic-camera feed for that? It was at the Elm, downtown. That's a reservations-only place so they might even have a record of it."

"Interesting," Eden muttered.

Rory muttered his agreement, and he took out his phone to text a question to Livvy. *Ask Ike about the knife he took from Helen.*

He watched as Livvy read the text, and then she turned her attention back to Ike. "I understand you were in an altercation with your former sister-in-law, Helen. Tell me about that."

"Altercation," Ike spluttered like it was a profanity. "More like all bark and no bite. Helen threatened me with a knife, and I knocked it out of her hand. I told her to leave or I'd call the cops and have her arrested for attempted assault with a deadly weapon. Not that you cops would have done anything about it," he grumbled. "But the threat worked. She tucked tail and got out of there fast."

"What did you argue about?" Livvy asked.

"Same ol', same ol'. You did my sister wrong. Boo-hoo. Helen hasn't learned how to shake off the past." But there was something in Ike's tone that made Eden believe Ike hadn't quite managed to shake it off, either.

"So you argued. Helen took out the knife, you grabbed it and she left," Livvy said, summarizing. "What happened then? What did you do with the knife?"

"I was going to throw it away, but then I thought maybe it'd sting for her to see it again. You know, a reminder that I bested her. So I put it in a plastic bag and had my assistant take it to her house. She wasn't home so he left it by her front door."

"Where anyone could have taken it," Eden muttered and then groaned.

"Your assistant will confirm he left it?" Livvy asked.

"Damn right, he will. He even got a picture of it, like delivery drivers do." Ike took out his phone, and after thumbing through his pictures, he pulled up the shot.

Eden couldn't see it from where she was standing, but judging from Livvy's expression, it was exactly what Ike had said it was.

"It was the damndest thing," Ike went on after Livvy requested that he forward the photo to her. "My assistant said as he was driving out of Helen's neighborhood he thought he saw Diedre. Not sure what she would have been doing there," he added in a mutter.

Eden looked at Rory, who was already taking out his phone. "I'm arranging a meeting with Diedre," he said. "I think it's time we chatted with her in person."

Eden thought so, too. Because if Ike was telling the

truth, then maybe the unthinkable had happened. Mercy. Had Diedre and Helen created an unholy alliance to go after a man they wanted to destroy?

When Rory finished his call, he turned to her. "Diedre says we can see her now. It'll take us about twenty-five minutes to get to her place. Are you game?"

"Absolutely." She glanced in the interview room. "Livvy will have to cut Ike loose soon, anyway, and I'd rather not be around for that."

Eden didn't mind having words with Ike, but it would be a waste of breath. Besides, she figured Arnette was on the verge of filing a complaint of police harassment, and it was better not to add any fuel to that.

The moment she and Rory were in the cruiser, Eden made a call to Leslie, putting it on speaker, and the nanny answered right away.

"We're all settled in," Leslie said. "And Tyler is having a blast with the toys in the playroom." As usual, the nanny sounded upbeat, but Eden still detected the worry. "Is everything okay with Rory and you?"

"We're on our way to interview a person of interest," Eden explained. "We just wanted to see how Tyler and you were doing."

"Listen for yourself," Leslie said, and she must have moved her phone closer to Tyler, because Eden could hear Tyler babbling. And laughing.

That did her heart good to hear her baby so happy. Thankfully, he was too young to understand what was going on.

"Grace and Dutton have been great," Leslie went on. "They've put Tyler in the nursery since baby Nash is still sleeping in their room. I'm in the guest suite directly across the hall from Tyler. I'll keep a close eye on him."

"Thank you," Eden and Rory said together.

It was Eden who continued, doling out the news that Leslie needed to know. "Ike will likely be released if he hasn't been already. We didn't have enough grounds to hold him."

Leslie stayed quiet a moment. "Dutton insisted his father wouldn't get near this place."

"And he won't." She hoped. "Just keep Tyler inside for a while, all right? Maybe it won't be long before we get all of this sorted out."

"Yes," Leslie muttered. "Stay safe," she added, and after saying their goodbyes, Eden ended the call.

Eden's sigh was a little louder than she'd intended, and Rory reached across the seat to take hold of her hand. Somehow, it seemed just as intimate as a kiss. And Eden welcomed it. Having their son in possible danger was bad enough, and she couldn't imagine going through this without Rory.

Since she had to get her mind off Tyler, Eden eased her hand from Rory's and used her phone to start getting some work done. She located the number for the Elm and called the restaurant.

It took her a couple of minutes to work her way up to the manager, but once she got through, it was confirmed that Diedre had indeed made reservations there. She got the info she needed from the manager, ended the call and then groaned.

"Five and a half months ago," she said to Rory. "That's when Diedre made a reservation for three at the Elm."

"Five and a half months," he repeated. He didn't groan. He cursed.

And she knew why. That was shortly before Mellie's murder.

It could be a coincidence. In fact, it probably was because she was still having a hard time imagining three of Ike's enemies plotting murder over a meal.

"I don't suppose the manager could recall anything about the lunch?"

Eden shook her head. "And they only keep security-cam feed for a week." She went to a search engine to see what she could find. "I'll look through social media to see if Diedre posted or was tagged in a photo of the lunch."

Though she was having a hard time imagining that as well. If this trio had been discussing anything remotely criminal, they likely wouldn't have wanted to document the occasion. And that's why Eden widened her search to anyone posting a photo from the Elm during the time and date of Diedre's reservation. Data mining could be a tedious process, but she'd gotten lucky a couple of times using this angle.

She looked up from her search and realized that Rory was firing glances in the rearview mirror. "Everything all right?" she asked, automatically turning to have a look.

"It's good. I'm just keeping an eye out," he assured her.

There were a couple of cars behind and in front of them now, but she couldn't see a threat. Then again, the threat could be there so she was glad Rory was staying vigilant. She did, too, while she continued her search.

"No photos or posts for the time of the reservation," she told Rory. "But Diedre is very active on social media. She has a lot of bad things to say about Ike." She continued to scan through the dozens of daily posts. "The woman documented most of her meals, the weather and even her schedule. She made it very easy for the killer to know exactly where she would be."

"Most meals," Rory repeated. "But not the one at the Elm."

No, she hadn't, and that in itself could be telling. However, it didn't make her a killer.

"More posts about Ike," she went on. And she reached the ones that would have been while Rory's mom was still alive.

Good grief. Diedre hadn't hidden the fact she was involved with a married man. She didn't specifically name him, but there were a few photos of her with Ike.

And that brought her back to her concerns about Rory.

"Are you okay with seeing Diedre?" she asked as he took the final turn toward her neighborhood.

"I'm never okay with it, but I can manage it," he insisted. "What I feel for Diedre is all rolled into the same ball with the grief over losing my mom."

His father's cheating was in the mix, too. Then again, Ike apparently did a lot of cheating over the years.

"I'm sorry," she said.

He shrugged. "Dealing with Diedre will be worth it if we get answers about the murders."

Yes, but that didn't mean this wouldn't put Rory through an emotional ringer. And that's the reason she gave his hand a squeeze as they drove into Quarry Heights, an upscale neighborhood on the far east edge of San Antonio. There was no security gate, though, so they were able to drive straight through to Diedre's. They got out, but before they even reached the front door, it opened, and a concerned-looking Diedre met them.

"I'm glad you came," she blurted, ushering them inside. "Please tell me you've arrested Ike."

"No," Rory answered.

Diedre groaned. "I was hoping you had good news. I thought that's why you wanted to see me."

Rory gave Diedre a glance before they followed her into

a living room that looked more like a showroom for expensive furnishings than an actual living space.

"No," he repeated. "We're here to ask you some questions. And before we start, I'm going to read you your rights."

That put some alarm in Diedre's eyes.

"It's for your protection," Rory informed her. He recited the Miranda warning. Then waited, no doubt to see if Diedre was going to demand a lawyer. When she didn't, he launched into the interview. "Tell us about the lunch you had at the Elm five and a half months ago."

Diedre had been in the process of sitting down on a silver leather sofa but that stopped her. She froze. Blinked. "Lunch at the Elm. Why would you want to know about that…?" She sank down onto the sofa and rolled her eyes. "Because Ike saw me there, and he told you. What did he say?"

"He recalled seeing you." That was all Rory admitted while Eden and he took the love seat across from Diedre. "Tell us about it," he repeated. "Who was there with you?"

Diedre took her time answering. "Helen and Brenda."

So she hadn't denied it, and Diedre still seemed confused as to why they would be questioning her about this.

"I'll be talking to Helen," Rory went on, "but could you tell me what the three of you discussed during the lunch?"

Diedre opened her mouth but didn't answer. Probably because of the sound of approaching footsteps. All of them turned in the direction of the arched entry, and Eden saw the woman step into view.

Helen.

What the heck was she doing there?

Rory's aunt didn't offer up any explanation. Or even

any kind of a greeting. The glances she gave Eden and him were laced with annoyance.

"So you two are friends now?" Rory asked Helen as she sat down on the sofa. Not right next to Diedre, but on the far end. "Because after Mom died, I recall you having some nasty things to say about Diedre."

"Rightfully so," Diedre murmured.

Helen shot the woman a glance and wasn't able to mask the venom that was still there. "I suppose you could say that Diedre and I have reached a truce because of our mutual hatred for Ike. He helped my sister into an early grave with the stress he put on her. And Ike has done his level best to destroy Diedre both personally and professionally."

"The enemy of my enemy is my friend," Diedre said. "I mean, it's the reason Mellie and I got close."

Eden had known that Diedre and Mellie sometimes talked, but she wasn't sure Mellie considered the woman an actual friend. She could be wrong about that, though, and Mellie and Diedre could have indeed bonded over Ike's mutual hatred for them and vice versa.

"And now Ike is trying to destroy me," Helen interjected. "Did he claim Diedre and I are setting him up for the murders?"

Neither Rory nor Eden responded to that, but Eden decided to backtrack a little, and she read Helen her rights just as Rory had done to Diedre. Helen didn't seem bothered by that, and she didn't request a lawyer. She just gave Eden a cool stare.

"Why was Brenda at the lunch with you two?" Eden asked once she'd finished with the Miranda.

"Another enemy of my enemy," Helen said quickly. "In fact, it was Brenda who wanted to meet with us. The lunch was all her idea."

"I made the reservation because I eat there often and already had the app on my phone," Diedre added. "But, yes, Brenda arranged it. She wanted to find out if there was a way to make Ike pay. Nothing criminal," she added.

"Then, what did she have in mind?" Rory replied.

Helen and Diedre exchanged a glance. "She wanted to hire someone, a PR expert, who could start a smear campaign. She had already tried to talk Mellie and Frank Mott into going along with it, too, but I think they both turned her down. That didn't stop Brenda, though." She paused. "Simply put, she wanted to ruin your father."

"And did you want that, too?" Rory asked.

"We did," Helen admitted.

"Yes," Diedre confirmed. "And we even tried a second time to encourage Mellie to join us." She turned her attention to Eden. "After all, Ike was horrible to her for years. But Mellie turned us down again."

Eden couldn't ask the question fast enough. "When was this?"

"A couple of days after the lunch," Helen offered. "Yes, the timing is terrible, isn't it? I mean with Mellie being murdered shortly thereafter."

The timing was indeed suspicious, and it made Eden wonder if Mellie had said something when she had turned them down. Something that had spooked Helen, Diedre or Brenda. If the three had brought up anything about framing Ike for a crime, no way would Mellie have gone along with that.

Had that been the reason Mellie was murdered?

Sweet heaven, it was possible.

"So why are you here now?" Rory asked, turning toward his aunt. "More planning on how to get back at Ike?"

Helen shook her head. "No, Diedre is worried about

being killed. It's obvious Ike is on a murder spree, and we're both in danger."

Eden wasn't so sure about Ike's involvement, but the spree part might be what was happening. Still, it didn't mean Ike was behind it. *The enemy of my enemy is my friend* didn't always pan out.

And that put Helen at the top of their suspect list.

"Tell me about the altercation you had with Ike," Rory said to his aunt. "The one that involved a knife."

Helen's mouth went tight. "Altercation? Is that what he called it?"

"No, a witness did," Rory replied.

"Dutton," Helen grumbled. "Well, if altercation is the label you want to put on it, fine, but it was just another round of Ike being Ike." She gathered her breath. "I stopped by the house to pick up a locket that I'd given my sister years ago. She'd given me an identical one, and I wanted the set as a memento. Ike started slinging insults at me, and when I felt threatened by him, I took out my knife."

"Threatened?" Eden asked. "How?"

"Getting in my face. Telling me I was a whiny brat." She paused. "And then he said my sister hated my guts, that she would make fun of me whenever I wasn't around."

Eden could see that the last insult had truly gotten to the woman. Even now, there was a mix of both anger and hurt on her face.

"My sister loved me, and I loved her," Helen went on, "and I was sick of Ike and his toxic ways. So I drew the knife, not intending to use it. For just a second, I wanted him to be afraid."

"And was he?" Eden persisted.

Helen shook her head, sighed. "No, he punched my

hand, and I dropped the knife. He picked it up, and I thought he was going to use it against me, so I left."

That meshed with the account Dutton had told them. Of course, Dutton hadn't known what Helen's actual motives were for pulling that knife. It was possible the woman had indeed planned on harming Ike.

"What happened to the knife?" Rory asked.

"I have no idea. You'd have to ask Ike about that." She stopped, the anger overtaking the hurt in her expression. "Is he using that knife to try to set me up?"

"As far as I know, there's no proof whatsoever that Ike or anyone else is trying to set you up," Rory told her.

That was true. No proof. But that didn't mean it wasn't happening.

Rory's phone dinged with a text, and when he glanced at it, he stood. "All right. If you recall anything else about that lunch or if Ike attempts to contact you, please let us know."

Helen didn't react to that, but Diedre seemed relieved that the questions were over. They were for now. But Eden figured they'd be talking to Helen and Diedre again very soon.

"That was a text from Sanchez, the CSI," Rory said once they were outside. "The bugs they found at Ike's were tapped into his Wi-Fi, and they've traced the output from the eavesdropping devices to an internet server."

"To Helen?" she asked.

He shook his head. "No, to Brenda."

Eden didn't bother to groan, and that meant the listening devices couldn't be used in the case against Ike.

Or Helen.

It was essentially a dead end, leaving them to speculate about what had possibly happened.

"So if we're to believe Helen and Diedre," Eden said as they got into the cruiser, "Brenda arranged that lunch to gain support to launch a smear campaign against Ike. She might or might not have gotten that support. Either way, she bought the burner and set up those fake texts that she was presumably going to make sure the police saw."

"She could have brought them in when asking for protection because she was in fear for her life," Rory suggested. "Then, she planted the bugs and waited until she was certain Ike didn't have an alibi, and she attacked Mellie."

Yes, Eden could see that playing out. Mellie wouldn't have been afraid of opening the door to Brenda.

"She waited for the cops to arrest Ike," Rory went on as he drove away from the house, "but when that didn't happen, she could have planned another attack on Helen or Diedre."

"But someone killed Brenda first," Eden said, finishing.

She would have said more had she not spotted the young blond-haired man by the subdivision gate. He was frantically trying to wave them down.

"Hell," Rory muttered. "I recognize him from his photo. That's the man who was stalking Brenda."

"Carter Rooney," Eden related. SAPD had interviewed him after Brenda's death, but Carter was also on the list of people they needed to see.

"Get your gun ready," Rory told her.

She did, and he pulled to a stop next to Carter, who immediately came closer. Rory didn't lower the window, and they both gave Carter a once-over. If he was carrying a weapon, he had it well hidden.

"Deputy McClennan?" he asked.

Rory nodded but still didn't put down the window.

"Good. Because I have something you need to see." The man took out his phone. "I believe I have proof that Diedre was the one who murdered Brenda."

Chapter Eight

Rory didn't look at the phone that Carter thrust at him. He kept his attention pinned to the man himself, waiting to see if this was a ruse to try to murder them.

After all, Carter was a person of interest in Brenda's murder. Had to be since there was a restraining order against him. But other than not having an alibi, SAPD hadn't found anything to hold him, and Rory hadn't gotten around to questioning him.

Well, he sure as heck had some questions now.

"Why are you here?" Rory demanded, and he lowered the window just a fraction so the man could hear him better, but not so wide that he could get the barrel of a gun through the opening.

"Oh," Carter said, suddenly not as eager as he had been just seconds earlier. "I've, uh, been keeping an eye on Diedre." He motioned toward a small pull-off area on the other side of the neighborhood sign. "I'm parked over there."

Since that explained exactly squat, Rory repeated the question. "Why are you here?"

Carter huffed and lowered his phone to the side of his leg. "Because I'm worried the cops might try to pin Brenda's murder on me. I didn't kill her," he added quickly, "but they asked me a bunch of questions, and they think I'm guilty. I could see it. It was all over their faces."

"They believe that because you were stalking Brenda," Rory pointed out. "Or do you deny that?"

The man took his time responding and finally shook his head. "No. I followed her around. I called her and left threatening messages."

"You stalked her," Eden snapped.

"Well, if I did, it was because she deserved it," he added without a pause. "She deserved worse. Brenda destroyed my business."

Rory had read all about that, and it was true. Well, it was mostly true, anyway. Because she had been friends with Carter's late mother, Brenda had loaned Carter about fifty grand to open a pub near the downtown River Walk. However, after Ike's antics had cost Brenda a good chunk of her income and customers, she had called in the loan. Carter had fought repaying it, but it was a fight he'd lost. And without any working revenue, the pub had gone belly up.

Yet another casualty of Ike's dirty dealings.

"I asked Brenda just to wait a couple more months, and then I could start repaying the loan," Carter went on. "But she wouldn't. She took me to court."

"Because she had no choice," Rory pointed out. "She was on the verge of having to declare bankruptcy."

"She had a choice," Carter practically shouted. "She could have gone into business with me. Then, we both would have had an income."

"Maybe," Eden said, "but that wasn't the decision Brenda made, and you stalked her because of it."

Carter looked ready to spew out some obscenities about Brenda, but he must have realized that wouldn't do him any good. He clearly had something he wanted them to see. Something on the phone he held in a white-knuckle grip.

"After I lost the pub," he went on, his voice and demeanor much calmer now, "I started following Brenda, looking for something I could use to have her arrested. I wanted her punished."

"You stalked her," Eden repeated, and it was obvious she had no sympathy for this guy. Neither did Rory.

"Yes, I've already admitted that," he said, still in the calm mode. "And after she got a restraining order, I kept my distance but continued to watch her through binoculars and the long-range lens of my camera." Now, he did pause. "I was watching her the night she was murdered. I think I saw when she was taken."

Everything inside Rory went on high alert. "You saw who took Brenda but didn't tell the cops?"

"No." Carter held up his hands in a stop gesture. "I didn't actually see the person. I saw a car speeding away from her place, and in hindsight I think she might have been in the vehicle. I'm not sure when she was attacked, but I believe the timing would fit. It was maybe around five p.m."

Yes, that *could* fit. Could. But Carter didn't seem at all certain of the time. Then again, he could be feigning uncertainty and knew the exact time that Brenda had been snatched or lured.

"Tell me what you saw," Rory demanded. "And then when you're done, I want you to cover both investigative bases by going first to SAPD and then to Renegade Canyon to give a full statement." SAPD would need to be involved since the possible abduction would have taken place in their jurisdiction.

Carter gave a shaky nod, and he didn't look at all sure

he would do that. Eden must have thought so, too, because Rory saw her send two texts. No doubt to someone at SAPD and at Renegade Canyon who'd make sure Carter showed up to tell them this latest information.

Or this lie.

Rory wasn't sure which.

"Like I said, I was watching Brenda's place," Carter explained, "but I must have fallen asleep because I didn't see the car go to her house. But I woke up when I heard an engine revving, and I saw it speed past me."

Rory huffed. "So you don't know if the vehicle was even at her place?"

"I think it was." There was more uncertainty, but then something lit up in his eyes. "But the car isn't what I wanted to tell you about." He dragged in a long breath. "I tried to follow the vehicle, but when I lost it, I decided to drive by here." He motioned to Diedre's house.

"Why?" Eden asked. She had finished her texts, put her phone on her lap and slid her hand back over the butt of her weapon in her holster.

"Because Brenda had been coming over here a lot, and I thought maybe the car was Diedre's." He lifted the phone again. "There was a car in her driveway. I'm not positive it was the same vehicle I saw leaving Brenda's, but I believe it could be."

Carter showed them the photo that he'd taken of a dark green Jeep. The heavily tinted windows made it impossible to see inside, but the man had gotten a shot of the license plate.

Eden immediately snatched up her phone again and ran a search on it. "The car's registered to Diedre."

Rory had to stop himself from rolling his eyes. "It's not a crime for a person to park their car in their own driveway."

"Yes, but I think a crime might have been committed. Look at this," Carter insisted, showing them another photo.

It was of a very harried-looking Diedre coming out of her house and heading back to the car. Her hair was scraped back in a messy ponytail, and she appeared to be fumbling with her keys.

"Notice what's she's wearing," Carter added.

Rory noted the woman's slim black pants and gray top. "So?"

"That wasn't the outfit she had on when she came home," Carter explained. "She was wearing this."

In the next photo he pulled up, Diedre was wearing baggy sweatpants and a T-shirt that looked like workout clothes. Again, there was no crime in someone changing clothes, but then Rory looked at the time stamp of the photo.

Eight p.m.

If Diedre had been the one to attack Brenda, that would have given her time to get to Renegade Canyon with Brenda, stab her and leave her in that barn to die.

Hell.

Had that happened?

Had Diedre taken this damn hit list so far that she'd murdered two women?

Rory not only didn't have answers for that, but he also had another question to add to it. "Why didn't you immediately take this to SAPD or to us?" he asked Carter.

"Because like I said, SAPD think I'm guilty. I don't want to go to them with anything. And when I saw your Renegade Canyon cruiser, I thought maybe you'd be more objective, that you'd believe in innocent until proven guilty. I'm not guilty," he added.

Maybe. Rory was going to hold out judgment on that.

Rory tipped his head to the man's phone. "Text us those photos," he instructed. "Then, show them to SAPD. It's possible these pictures can clear your name," Rory added when he saw the hesitancy in Carter's eyes. "The time stamps could show you weren't near Brenda when she was attacked."

Of course, it might show just the opposite, but Rory was going to keep that to himself.

He rattled off his phone number to Carter, and the man began forwarding the photos to Rory's phone. Rory passed his phone to Eden so she could have a closer look and send them to the county crime lab for analysis. Of course, SAPD would be doing the same thing, but it wouldn't hurt to have two sets of eyes on these.

"One more thing," Rory went on, aiming a hard stare at Carter. "If you don't show up at SAPD within the hour, they'll come looking for you, and it'd be best if that didn't happen."

Carter gave another of those unconvincing nods, and he'd just finished sending the pictures when his gaze whipped in the direction behind the cruiser. Rory looked in his side mirror and saw Diedre heading their way.

"I have to go," Carter blurted, and the man took off running toward his car.

Rory considered going after him, but with Diedre and Carter as suspects, he decided for now to leave Carter to SAPD. Renegade Canyon PD could get a crack at him later.

"I'll give SAPD a heads-up about the photos," Eden murmured, taking care of that while Diedre stepped up alongside the cruiser.

"What's going on?" Diedre demanded, stooping down and staring at them through the window. "Why are you still here, and who is that man?"

Rory debated how much to say, and he decided to see how Diedre would react to Carter's accusations. "It's come to my attention that there was some unusual activity at your house the night Brenda was attacked."

Diedre's frown deepened, and she glanced at Carter, who was now speeding away. "That man told you something about me? Who is he?"

Rory didn't intend to spill that since Diedre might go after him. "Was your Jeep parked in your driveway at any time in the past twenty-four hours?"

Diedre froze for a couple of moments. "Why?"

"Just answer the question," Rory ordered.

After a long hesitation, she nodded. "I believe it was."

"But you don't know for sure?" Rory persisted.

She made another glance at the spot where she'd seen Carter speeding away. "Yes, I parked in my driveway in the afternoon, maybe around four o'clock or a little later. I, uh, had left for the gym for a workout, but I realized I'd forgotten my membership card so I had to go back in my house to get it."

"And then what did you do?" Rory continued.

Diedre's forehead creased. "What did that man tell you?"

Rory ignored that and repeated his question, causing Diedre to huff.

"I went to the gym," she snapped. "I had a long workout."

"What's the name of your gym?" Eden asked.

The alarm went through Diedre's eyes again. "I didn't actually work out in the gym. I decided to use the outdoor track. I jogged about four miles, sat for a while and then walked some before I came home."

It was possible Diedre was telling them she'd done that walking around to cover for time she was gone. Time when she could have been attacking Brenda.

"And you parked in your driveway again," Rory said. It wasn't a question.

Diedre nodded. "My garage-door app wasn't working so, yes, I left my car in the driveway. Why?" she asked.

"Just routine questions." Of course, that was a lie, and this entire conversation would have to be put in a report with a copy sent to SAPD. "Did you wear your workout clothes home from your walk?"

Again, Diedre took her time answering, and Rory didn't think it was his imagination that the woman was about to lawyer up. If so, that would put a quick end to his questions. "Yes," she finally said.

"When did you change? You said you didn't use the gym," he reminded her.

This time, it was more than concern in her eyes. It was anger. "I changed in my car," she growled, "and I left on my workout clothes because I'd spilled a sports drink on my other outfit."

"And what happened to that outfit?" Rory asked.

Diedre stepped back. "This conversation is over," she snarled, and she turned and headed back to her house.

"I'll make another call to SAPD," Eden said as they watched Diedre storm off. "I'll see if they can get a search warrant for her house."

It was a necessary step in the investigation, but it would likely be too late. If Diedre had stabbed Brenda while wearing those clothes, then the top and pants had probably been destroyed, or trashed. Still, SAPD might get lucky and find something else they could use to build the case against Diedre.

Against Carter, too.

Because it was possible he was the killer and had given them the photos to toss the blame onto someone else.

Rory raised his window and started driving back toward Renegade Canyon while Eden dealt with getting that search warrant. As expected, it wasn't a fast process, and they were nearly halfway home before she finished.

"Detective Vernon will get right on the warrant for both Diedre's house and Jeep," Eden informed him. "And he'll make sure Carter comes in. I'll go ahead and forward Vernon a copy of the photos just in case Carter decides to delay that visit."

"Good idea." Because Carter was spooked. Or else just guilty. Rory didn't know which.

He heard the swooshing sound of her phone to let him know the photos had gone out. "I went ahead and sent them to the lab, too," she added, and she began to study the pictures.

Rory glanced at her and saw she had enlarged the area around the Jeep windows, no doubt trying to see if anyone was inside. Judging from her sigh, she couldn't manage that.

"I'm not seeing any blood or tears on either set of clothes," Eden muttered. "Nothing to indicate she'd had these on during the attack." She stopped. "But if she managed to drug Brenda, maybe there was no actual struggle."

Yeah, Rory had gone there, too. "Since Brenda and Diedre had that semifriendship deal, they could have met. Diedre could have given her the drug, and then once it kicked in, she could have led Brenda to her Jeep. And even into the barn. No lifting required."

Though that did leave them with a huge question. One that Eden voiced.

"Then, if she had Brenda drugged and in her Jeep, why would Diedre have returned to her house around four p.m.?"

Rory could only speculate about that. "Maybe she hadn't

drugged Brenda yet, and Diedre was on the way to meet Brenda when she remembered she had indeed forgotten something at her house."

Maybe the search warrant could give them something else to work with to confirm or dispel that theory. The search should include a check of Diedre's GPS so they could track where the woman had been.

Eden muttered an agreement and continued to look at the photos. Rory made occasional glances at her, but once he was off the highway and onto the rural road that led to Renegade Canyon, he had to keep watch around them. Eden and he had possibly rattled some cages today with Diedre, Helen and Carter, and that rattling could have made the killer desperate to silence them.

Not a comforting thought.

Eden made a sharp sound of surprise, causing Rory's attention to zoom in her direction. It wasn't something she spotted outside the cruiser but rather in one of the photos.

"It's Frank," Eden blurted.

She held up the photo that Carter had taken of Diedre's Jeep speeding away from her house. Eden had enlarged not the Jeep, but the area on the other side of the street. There, tucked in along a cluster of cedar trees, stood Frank.

What the hell was he doing there?

"Should I call him and see if he's home?" Eden asked. "We could stop by there and have a chat with him."

"Do that," Rory agreed even though it was a possibility the picture had been altered to add Frank's image. But that only led to another question.

Why would Carter have done that?

Frank was a potential victim, not a suspect. At least he hadn't been until Rory had seen this picture.

Yeah, he definitely wanted to talk to Frank, and then Detective Vernon could do the same with Carter.

"Frank's not answering his phone," Eden said, and then she left a voice mail for the man to contact them right away.

Rory would give him an hour, and then he intended to track Frank down. If the man had any connection to these murders, then Rory needed to know.

"I'll reach out to the lab and light a fire, see if they can get working on the photos sooner rather than later," Eden said, making that call.

Rory had to slow down as he approached a curve that had earned the nickname of Dead Man's Bend, since over the years, it had been the site of two fatal car crashes. He came out the steep curve and immediately spotted something on the road.

Hell.

It was a strip of metal spikes stretched across the asphalt. A strip meant to take out the tires of a vehicle and bring it to a stop.

It sure as hell shouldn't have been there.

Rory slammed on the brakes. But he was too late. He hit the strip, the spikes ripping through the tires and causing him to lose control. It was like having four blowouts at once. He had to fight the steering wheel just to stay on the road.

But even that became impossible.

Because of the second strip of spikes.

The cruiser ran over it, and this time there was the sound of the metal spikes gouging into the tire barrels and rims. The vehicle skidded and another jolt slung them around.

Finally, the cruiser came to a complete stop. And in that blink, Eden and he were now sitting ducks.

Rory drew his gun and waited for the attack.

Chapter Nine

Eden drew her gun, too, and she fired glances all around them. She expected gunfire, but she couldn't see a shooter, only the thick woods that were on both sides of the road.

Woods where a killer could hide and lie in wait.

No way had kids done this. A spike strip wasn't easy to come by, and she knew in her gut, this wasn't a prank. It was a way to pin them in place while someone moved in for the kill.

Not Diedre, or even Helen, since Rory had taken the shortest route possible for the return trip home, and neither woman could have gotten ahead of them. But either or both of the women could have hired someone to do this. The same could be said for their other suspects, Ike, Frank and even Carter.

Any one of them could be responsible.

"Siri, call police dispatch," Rory instructed his app, and the sound of his voice cut through the heavy silence that'd settled inside the cruiser. The dispatcher answered on the first ring.

"This is Deputy Rory McClennan," he said. "I'm requesting immediate backup to the Old Sawmill Road about a half mile from the east side of the bridge on Dead Man's Bend. My cruiser has been disabled by two spike strips stretched across the road. Tell responding officers to approach with caution."

"I'll get someone out there right away," the dispatcher assured him, and Rory ended the call.

Eden knew it would probably take only about ten minutes for one of their fellow deputies to respond, but those minutes would feel like an eternity. Added to that, the only risk wasn't from a possible shooter.

No.

They were on the back end of Dead Man's Bend, which was essentially a steep, blind curve. The cruiser was straddling the center line of the road with no shoulder to speak of that could be used as an emergency lane. They could be hit by another vehicle, and delivery trucks used this route to bring supplies into town.

The cruiser was bullet-resistant, but it certainly wouldn't withstand a head-on collision with a semitruck.

Eden listened for any possible threat. An oncoming vehicle. A shooter. But she heard and saw nothing.

Maybe this was the attack, having them locked in place like this. If the attacker had done some research, then they might have learned if a truck was indeed heading their way. No more would need to be done to either seriously injure or kill them. And the attacker could simply just walk away.

"Open your door just a fraction," Rory instructed. He was not only glancing all around them, but he also had his head lifted and was listening. "Not enough so that a shot can get through. But keep it open in case we have to run from the cruiser."

That definitely wasn't something she wanted to do. Because a shooter could just gun them down. Still, they might not have a choice in the matter if they were about to be struck by another vehicle.

She opened her door less than an inch while he gave the voice command to the phone app again, making a second call to Dispatch.

"Alert responding officers and any and all traffic that my cruiser is disabled in the center of the road," Rory said the moment he was on the line.

The dispatcher would no doubt do her best to make that alert, but it would be next to impossible to get out the word to everyone.

"Also remind any responders that there could be a shooter or explosives in the area," Rory added.

"Explosives," she muttered.

Dreading what she might see, Eden looked out the window and down at the part of the spike strip and road that was in her line of sight.

And her heart sank.

She'd been so intent on checking the woods for an attacker or listening for a truck that she hadn't thought to look for a threat much closer to them.

"I think there's an IED on the spike strip just a couple of inches outside my door," she said to Rory.

He scrambled over the console to have a look. Rory was right in her face, so she had no trouble seeing the confirmation in his eyes. He immediately pulled away, scrambling back to his own side to gaze out his side.

And he cursed.

"There's one here, too," he said.

The adrenaline had already been slamming through her, but that bit of info gave her another round of it. Something she definitely didn't need. Her body was already in the fight-or-flight mode, and she couldn't do either.

"Are there explosives?" the dispatcher asked.

"Yes. Get the bomb squad out here now," Rory ordered, "and block off the road in both directions."

"Will do," the dispatcher said before ending the call.

Again, that was going to be a long shot to accomplish the roadblock. Things like that took precious time, and anyone who did respond to block it off could be walking straight into an ambush.

"I don't see a timer or detonator on the IED," Rory muttered.

"Neither do I," Eden acknowledged. "So maybe it's like the one at the barn. If we step on it, it goes off."

He made a sound of agreement and looked her in the eyes again. "If we have to get out, jump over the IED that's on your side of the cruiser, but watch where you step. There could be other devices."

She got another rush of adrenaline, and Eden had to try to stop the worst-case scenarios from playing out in her head. If she and Rory were both killed, Tyler would be an orphan. He could lose both of his parents in a blink.

And for what?

So a killer could throw chaos into the murder investigation? Or was this more personal than that?

She thought of their names being on Ike's hit list. A list that Brenda might have composed simply to set up Ike. But what if she hadn't done that? What if the killer had been the one to set her up?

If so, the list could be real.

With Rory and her the targets.

That thought was flashing through her head, but Eden forced herself to focus on a backup plan. Rory was clearly doing the same.

"If someone starts shooting at us," he said, "don't try to

return fire. Shut your door and get down. Because a bullet could set off the IED."

Definitely not something she wanted to happen.

As close as the IEDs were to them, the cruiser would be blown up. Maybe they would be, too. But at least there was a chance the cruiser would protect them enough so they could stay alive.

"If you hear an approaching vehicle," he went on, "try to get out and dive to the side of the road."

Again, not something she wanted to happen. Not with the threat of a shooter or more IEDs.

The seconds crawled by, and when her lungs started to ache, Eden had to remind herself to breathe. Had to try to settle her heartbeat, too, because it was thudding in her ears, blocking out too many sounds.

But she did hear one sound.

A welcome one.

It was a police siren, and it was coming from the direction of town. Seconds later, they got a call from Livvy.

"Are you two all right?" Livvy asked the moment Rory took the call on speaker.

"Been a whole lot better," Rory replied. "Are you solo?"

"No. Bennie's with me. We're about three minutes out. What will we be up against when we get to you?"

Rory huffed. "Not sure, but for certain there are two IEDs and two spike strips. Slow down well before you get to Dead Man's Bend."

Livvy muttered some profanity. "We're working on the roadblock," she explained. "But it's not in place yet."

Which meant the worst-case scenario could kick in.

"No sign of who did all this?" Bennie asked.

"None," Rory replied. "And I can't see a vehicle on either of the two trails that are visible from where we're stuck." He paused. "It's too risky for you to come close to us. You'll have to wait for the bomb squad."

"Understood," Livvy murmured, and there was a whole lot of regret about this in her voice. "But Bennie and I can help if there's gunfire."

"No, you can't," Rory said quickly. "All a shooter has to do is hit the IED with a bullet, and the whole area can blow up." He stopped, gathered his breath. "For now, just stop anyone from coming closer and plowing into us because that can detonate the IEDs, too."

Livvy cursed again. "All right," she said, and Eden didn't think it was her imagination that Livvy was trying to steady herself. "Once we have a visual on you, I stop and we wait." She paused. "ETA on the bomb squad is fifteen minutes."

Eden was surprised it was that short amount of time. The bomb squad was a county unit, and they were based in a town on the other side of Renegade Canyon.

"Sit tight. We'll be there soon," Livvy added before she ended the call.

The silence came again, but Eden had thankfully tamped down enough of her body's reactions so she could hear better. And she continued to keep watch since she didn't want a shooter darting out from the woods for a sneak attack. After all, the plan might not be to kill them here, but rather to take them elsewhere so their bodies could be staged like Mellie's and Brenda's.

With the barn gone and the CSIs still crawling all over the site, the killer might have to find a new location, though. But there were plenty of other barns that might be a good substitute.

Every muscle in her body went on alert when she heard something.

The sound of an engine.

"Hell, it's not Livvy and Bennie," Rory groaned.

No, it wasn't. This sound was coming from the opposite direction, and it didn't take long before the vehicle rounded the curve.

Sweet heaven.

It was a Mack truck.

"Move now," Rory shouted, and they reached for their doors at the same time.

Eden shoved open her door, hurdling over the IED and praying. She was doing so much praying. She dived to the ground on the side of the road. There was a steep slope, and she didn't have time to look for IEDs.

Or anything else, for that matter.

When she hit the ground, she just kept moving. Kept sliding down, down, down. So fast. And she couldn't stop before her arm slammed into a tree. The pain shot through her, from head to toe.

And her gun went flying.

So did plenty of other things.

Eden heard the sickening screech of tires. Heard the impact, too, of the Mack slamming into the cruiser. Metal crunching metal.

Then, the explosion.

The horrible blast tore through the air, shaking the very ground beneath her and knocking her into the tree again.

Her training kicked in. Her survival instincts, too, and she forced herself to get up so she could grab her gun. The thoughts and fears were slamming into her now.

So many thoughts.

So many fears.

For the driver of that truck. Of the possible IEDs that could be planted around her. Of a killer who could be waiting to strike. But there was one thought that stood out above all others, and it was screaming through her head.

Rory.

She had to get to Rory.

Keeping watch where she stepped, Eden scrambled back up the slope. Not easily. It was one step forward and two steps back in some places, but she finally made it up to the top.

And her heart went into overdrive.

It was a war zone. Parts of the truck and the cruiser were everywhere. The cab of the truck was still intact, though, thrown yards away from the collision, and she could see the driver, bleeding but still held in place by his seat belt.

He'd need medical attention right away, but Livvy and Bennie would be calling for an ambulance. They could deal with the driver. She had to get to Rory.

"Rory?" she called out, silently cursing when she realized her voice had almost no sound. Not enough breath.

Dodging the debris and hoping she didn't step on another IED, she made her way across to the other side of the road. Eden was about to make another attempt to call out to him...

But then she saw him.

There was blood on his head. On his arm, too. But he was alive and moving up the slope toward her.

Eden went to him, and she let relief claim every part of her body and soul. She pulled Rory into her arms and held on tight.

Chapter Ten

Rory sat in the back of the cruiser with Eden while Livvy drove them to his family's ranch. He figured it was going to be a long time before the tension in his muscles eased up. And it was going to be a hell of a lot longer than that before he'd feel comfortable letting Eden out of his sight.

Thankfully, she seemed to feel the same way, and once they'd been checked out at the hospital and done the nightmare of paperwork that came with something like this, she hadn't put up any argument about going to Dutton's with him.

Part of that was no doubt because she wanted to see Tyler. So did he. He desperately needed to be with their little boy and make sure for himself that he was okay. Again, Eden had to be of a like mind. But no matter what her reasoning, Rory would be able to keep an eye on both her and their son.

Even though it was already getting dark, there was enough dim light coming from the dash for him to see the fresh bruise on her chin. No stitches this time, but he'd heard the nurse say that Eden had bruises on her right arm and leg. He had some scrapes and bruises as well, but they were blessedly minor for both of them. It could have been much, much worse.

They'd come damn close to dying.

Again.

And once again the killer hadn't cared squat about their lives or any collateral damage from that IED blast. No one had died this time with this attack, but the driver of that Mack truck, Arlo Jenkins, had serious enough injuries that he'd had to be medevacked to a hospital in San Antonio. Arlo had simply been trying to do his job and make a delivery to a store in town when he'd driven over that IED.

Livvy pulled to a stop in front of Dutton's, and Rory spotted two ranch hands in a truck on the other side of the driveway. They were probably armed and ready in case the killer showed up here.

Dutton had taken other precautions, too. There had been two more hands in another truck positioned by the gated entrance, and two others were patrolling the grounds. The external security system was on as well, and while it wouldn't be impossible for someone to sneak onto the ranch, the sensors and motion-activated cameras would make it a little harder to approach undetected.

Livvy turned toward them, resting her left arm on top of the steering wheel, and she looked back at them through the metal grating that separated the front and back seats. "Damn," she muttered. "You two look like you lost a fight with a couple of heavyweight champions."

Close. They'd lost a fight with a killer. A killer who possibly had been long gone even before the cruiser ran over those spike strips. Added to that, they couldn't rule out any of their suspects as being responsible.

Livvy added a sigh. "Get some rest," she said as he and Eden got out of the cruiser.

Muscles that he didn't even know he had protested the simple movement. Not a searing pain, thank goodness, but both of them would likely have to deal with the soreness for a while. The impact of hitting those spike strips had been the equivalent of a collision. And then there'd been the falls down the slopes.

Yeah, there'd be lots and lots of discomfort.

Muttering their thanks and goodbyes to Livvy, they walked up the porch steps to Dutton's massive house, where seemingly every light was on. Dutton let them in, and the moment they stepped inside, they saw Grace standing to the side.

With Tyler.

Since it was past his bedtime, his son had sleepy eyes, but Rory was glad Grace and Dutton had kept him awake.

"Mama, Dada," Tyler babbled, lunging for Rory, who caught him and immediately adjusted his position so he could get hugs from both parents.

Just that hug eased a whole lot of the aches in his body. Relieved plenty of stress, too. Things had been touch and go during the attack, but Eden and he had had a lot to fight for. This. Their precious little boy.

"I've been reading the reports of what happened," Grace said. "But we can get into all of that in the morning. We can get into a lot of things tomorrow," she added. "There's lasagna in the fridge if you haven't had dinner."

"Thanks, but Livvy had some burgers brought from the diner while we were writing up our statements," Rory explained.

Not that Eden had eaten much. And he hadn't pressed her on that, either, since he figured her stomach was just as unsettled as his was.

Grace nodded. "All right, but if you get hungry, help yourself to anything in the kitchen. For now, I want you two to get some sleep. And that's an order," she said firmly, the concern all over her face and in her voice.

The concern was there from Dutton, too, and he used his phone to reset the security system while giving Rory the once-over. "We'll catch this—" He stopped, barely cutting off what would have been a word that Tyler shouldn't be hearing. "Person," Dutton said, finishing his thought.

"Yeah, we will," Rory responded, and he wasn't just blowing smoke. They *had* to catch the killer. There was no other choice. Because until they did, no one was safe.

Not even their baby.

"Tyler's been fed, bathed and he's ready for bed," Grace told them. "Leslie's in the guestroom, and she has the monitor. She said just to let her know when she should turn it on so you two can get some sleep."

Rory would be letting the nanny know that she wasn't on duty tonight because he would be staying with Tyler. He'd sacrifice a good night's sleep for the peace of mind that it'd give him to be in the room with his son.

"Nash is down for who knows how long so Dutton and I are going to catch some z's while we can," Grace added. She gave them gentle hugs before she and Dutton headed up the stairs toward the main bedroom.

Eden and Rory were right behind them, and Tyler leaned toward his mom so she could take him into her arms. She kissed the top of his head and held him close for several long moments. When they reached the nursery, she handed Tyler to Rory so he could do the same.

Since Tyler was rubbing his eyes now and fussing a little, Rory eased him into the crib, and he turned on his favorite mobile—horses—that someone had obviously brought over from Eden's. They both kissed Tyler again, and Rory texted Leslie to let her know there was no need for her to turn on the monitor.

Leslie quickly responded with a thumbs-up and a question. Are Eden and you all right?

No. They weren't. They were shaken to the core and nowhere closer to IDing the killer. But Rory went with a thumbs-up emoji of his own.

They stood by Tyler's crib until the boy drifted off to sleep. Even then, they didn't move. Maybe exhaustion was playing into that because Rory seemed frozen in place, and he might have just stood there all night had Eden not turned to him. In a blink, she pulled him into her arms.

"I thought you'd been blown up," she muttered, her voice cracking.

He'd thought the same about her, and Rory had experienced a mountain of relief when he had seen her coming down that slope toward him. And when she had dragged him into her arms, well, that'd been priceless.

Just as this hug was now.

Rory wasn't naive enough to believe that those hugs would erase all the barriers between them, but he couldn't help believing it was a start. They certainly felt like a unit. Like old times. And the old times escalated significantly when Eden eased back, and their gazes locked.

They stared at each other, and he saw her lips part as she sucked in a quick breath. He was doing some faster breathing, too, and his heart had revved up.

A lot of things had revved up.

And they just kept heading in that direction when they moved toward each other at the same time. Their mouths met, already desperate and hungry for what a kiss could give them.

And the kiss could give a whole lot.

Heat, comfort and oh, so much pleasure.

Rory dived right into the kiss. Right into the heat. And he let the taste and feel of her slide through him. Talk about a cure for all those aches and soreness. A cure for the nightmarish flashbacks, too. This kiss made him feel as if everything was right with the world.

It was temporary, of course. He knew that reality would soon set in. But for now, he just took everything Eden was offering him, and she was offering a hell of a lot.

She pressed her body against his. Her breasts to his chest. Center to center. He did some pressing, too, tightening his grip around her while staying mindful of her injuries. If she was feeling any pain, though, she wasn't showing it.

Eden made a sound of pleasure that he knew all too well, and it hiked up the heat even more. Rory notched it up further by deepening the kiss, by pressing even more against her.

Of course, the pleasure took on an edge, as it always did. An urgent, demanding one that in the past would have sent them in the direction of the nearest bed. Or wall. Or floor. Location hadn't always been high on their list of priorities. Only the release from this pressure cooker of heat.

But that couldn't happen now.

And Eden seemed to remember that at the same time he did because she pulled back from him. Her breath was gusting out now, and he could see she was fighting hard to rein herself in. She got some reinforcement on that when she glanced down into the crib. Tyler was still asleep, but it was best if he didn't wake up and see his parents having sex. Added to that, Rory wasn't even sure Eden was physically ready for sex. She needed rest.

And some pain meds.

Rory forced himself to move away from her, but not before he gave her a somewhat chaste kiss on the cheek. As chaste a kiss as it could be, considering their history. To avoid the temptation of pulling her right back into his arms, he went to the en suite bathroom and saw the ibuprofen that Grace or Dutton had already set out for them.

That wasn't the only thing his brother and sister-in-law had done, though. There were overnight bags for both Eden and him, things that had obviously been gathered from their houses, along with some bottles of water, bags of snacks and even a jar of bath salts on the side of the tub.

Making a mental note to thank Dutton and Grace in the morning, Rory took two of the tablets, got two more from the bottle, along with one of the waters, and brought them to Eden.

"Thanks," she whispered, and while she was downing them, Rory went to the closet and took out a pillow and a blanket.

"I'll sleep in the chair tonight," he said, tipping his head to a recliner in the sitting area. Across from it was a sofa that he knew pulled out into a bed. "You can take that or use one of the guestrooms." There were three of them, not counting the one Leslie was using, and two were on this floor.

"I'm sleeping in here," she insisted.

Rory had no intention of arguing with her about that. Yes, the guest bed would be a lot more comfortable, but she likely wouldn't get much sleep unless she could be close to Tyler.

Eden glanced at the bathroom. "But I would like a shower first."

"Take a long one," he suggested. "I'll do the same once you're finished."

She nodded, gave him a lingering look and headed toward the bathroom.

Rory silently cursed. The kiss had fueled that blasted need inside him. A need that made him forget all about his sore muscles and his banged-up body. And it took a whole lot of willpower not to follow Eden into the bathroom and finish what they'd started.

Instead, he forced himself to get a bed ready for her. Rory pulled out the sofa, took another pillow and blanket from the closet and put them on the mattress. He did the same to the recliner that was already positioned so he'd be able to see both Eden and the crib throughout the night.

The door, too.

And while he doubted the killer would come bursting in, he locked the door, anyway, and checked outside the window. Rory saw the men still guarding the house and the truck with the other hands driving around the ranch, checking for any signs of trouble while also monitoring the external security.

Satisfied that they were as secure as they could be, Rory put his phone on vibrate so the ringer wouldn't wake Tyler, and he went back to the recliner. He heard the water running in the bathroom, and he hoped Eden did as he suggested and took that long shower. While he waited for her, he used his phone to access his inbox to see if there were any updated reports.

There were.

Loads of them.

And the updates would no doubt continue throughout the night. There were many moving parts to this investigation, with two crime scenes, way too many suspects and three dead. Mellie, Brenda and Lou.

Rory didn't want anyone else added to that tally.

The first update was from Bennie, who, among other things, had been tasked with trying to locate Frank. So far, Bennie was having no luck whatsoever with that. Frank hadn't responded to multiple calls, and he hadn't answered his door when a reserve duty officer had gone to his residence. It was possible the man was simply avoiding them, but Rory could think of other reasons.

Bad ones.

If Frank was the killer, then he could be lying low after setting those IEDs and spike strips on the road. And Rory had to tamp down the anger that bubbled inside him when he thought of Frank, or anyone else, doing that. Getting revenge against Ike had already caused so much damage.

Out of all their suspects, Frank was the one who had the means to do something like that. Since he was from Renegade Canyon, he knew that road, knew the best place to set up a deadly attack. And now that he had seemingly dropped off the map, he couldn't supply them with an alibi.

Rory glanced through the background check on Frank, and while he couldn't see any experience with explosives, the man had served seven years in the Air Force, and it was possible he'd tapped into some skill he'd learned there. Of course, it was equally possible that Frank had hired someone. The man wasn't rich like Ike, Helen or Diedre, but he had more than enough assets to pay someone.

Rory moved to the next update—this one from the bomb squad—and again, it wasn't good news. There was no obvious signature on the IEDs. No trace, DNA or prints, either, that could help identify who'd made them. So that was a dead end.

The next report was on the photos that they'd gotten from Carter. According to the lab, the images hadn't been doctored. So Frank had indeed been at Diedre's when the woman had sped away in her Jeep.

The time stamp on the photos didn't clear either Frank or Carter as far as giving them an alibi since Brenda was almost certainly alive at the time the photos had been taken. That meant either man could have had time to leave Diedre's, get to Brenda, stab her and leave her to die in the barn.

So, yeah, not stellar news there.

The next report did offer a glimmer of something more positive. Carter had indeed gone into both Renegade Canyon PD and SAPD to give his statements, and he'd told SAPD Detective Vernon about the photos, which were now also at their crime lab. Vernon had used the info to obtain a search warrant for Diedre's car, home and office. The warrant would be executed in the morning and a team of CSIs would be looking for anything that could point to her being the killer.

Rory wished the detective could get a warrant for Helen's place, too, but he had no evidence against her that would help in that area. Still, he couldn't shut out the images of his aunt orchestrating all of this to get back at Ike.

And, yes, that included killing Eden and him.

Ike might have plenty of ill will toward Dutton, Eden and him, but it would still be a deep cut if someone murdered his family to get back at him. Plus, Helen might not find it any great loss to kill off her sister's children since she blamed them for not doing enough to save their mother.

Killing Eden and him would accomplish something else, too. It could throw the investigation into a tailspin.

The next report he pulled up was from the medical examiner, stating that the blade that'd killed Brenda could indeed have come from a Swiss Army knife. Rory sighed.

Because that put Ike right back in the center of suspicion. According to Dutton, Helen had threatened Ike with such a knife, and Ike had taken it from her. Ike would need to be questioned about that.

Rory looked up from the report and sighed when he heard Eden coming back into the room. Clearly, she hadn't opted for the long shower, and there was still a lot of tension in her eyes. But at least she was dressed for bed in loose joggers and a T-shirt.

He considered pulling her back into his arms but knew that was a bad idea. Instead, he tipped his head to the sofa. "Get some rest. I won't be long in the shower."

And he wasn't. He didn't want to leave Eden and Tyler alone, so he hurried, ignoring his protesting muscles. Rory didn't go with sleepwear, though. He put on some clean jeans and a black T-shirt just so he'd be ready if anything went wrong during the night.

When he went back into the nursery, Eden was already on the sofa bed and was in the process of putting her phone on vibrate. Once she'd done that, she lay down and gave him a long look before lifting the portion of the blanket that was on the empty side of the bed.

"I know it's a lot to ask, but I want you next to me," she muttered. "It's the only way I'll get any sleep."

"It's not a lot to ask at all." Rory put his holster on the end table.

He wanted to do this for her. Needed it. Yes, it would be torture having her so close but not kissing her. Or making love to her. But she didn't need kisses or sex. She just needed him.

So that's what he gave her.

Rory slid in next to her and eased Eden into his arms.

Chapter Eleven

Eden woke, slowly, parts of her seemingly protesting the mere opening of her eyes. But other parts alerted her to the warm, solid man pressed against her.

Rory.

She knew his scent and the feel of him. And those certain parts of her suddenly wanted more. Eden looked at him, to see if he was awake. He was, and her gaze collided with his intense brown eyes. They didn't move toward each other, but Eden was certainly thinking about doing that when she heard two sounds.

"Mama, Dada," Tyler babbled. He had pulled himself to a standing position in the crib and was smiling at them.

Eden automatically smiled back, and then she realized there was another sound. Rory's phone was vibrating and was practically dancing across the end table. She glanced at the time. Barely 7:00 a.m., which meant this almost certainly wasn't good news.

"It's Bennie," Rory revealed, groaning. "I'll take the call if you want to see to Tyler."

She definitely wanted to go to their son, and Eden understood why Rory didn't put the call on speaker. There was no telling what gruesome details of the investigation Bennie might mention.

Tyler gave her a sloppy kiss, and he tightened his arms around her neck when she picked him up. Just that slight pressure caused some discomfort, but no way would she loosen his grip. She needed this contact. This moment with him.

Eden held Tyler, and he babbled his way to the changing table, where there were plenty of supplies. Not just diapers and wipes, but extra clothes for their son, too.

While she changed him, she looked back at Rory. One glimpse at his expression, and she got confirmation that something bad had happened.

Please, not another murder.

But with the killer unidentified and therefore at large, it was possible he'd struck again.

She finished changing Tyler just as Rory ended the call. "Let's take Tyler to Leslie," he said, giving the baby a kiss, "and then we can talk."

Eden didn't press him for info. She stepped into the hall and practically ran right into Leslie.

"Me," Tyler squealed, which was as close as he'd come to saying the nanny's name. When he reached for her, Leslie took him into her arms. She also studied Eden's face for a moment.

"Rory just got a work call," Eden explained.

Leslie nodded, and even though she must have noticed Eden's dour expression, she managed to smile at Tyler. "Let's go downstairs and get some oatmeal," she offered.

"Me, me, me," Tyler gushed, using a slightly different inflection from what he'd called Leslie.

Eden sneaked in another quick kiss to Tyler's cheek, and then she went back into the nursery. Rory had already put on his boots and was in the process of strapping on his shoulder holster.

"About an hour ago, Dispatch received an anonymous call saying there was a body by the welcome sign for town. Judson and Garrison responded," he said, referring to their fellow deputies, Judson Docherty and Garrison Zimmer, who was a rookie. "And they did indeed find a body." He paused. "It's Carter."

Eden had to do a mental double take, and she shook her head. "Carter?" she repeated. "Does Ike even know him?"

"We'll soon find out because when Judson and Garrison got to the scene, Ike was there," Rory explained.

Oh, mercy. "Did Ike kill him?"

Rory groaned and scrubbed his hand over his face. "To be determined. I'm going out there now, but if you'd rather stay here—"

"I'll get dressed and go with you." Yes, part of her did want to stay with Tyler, but this was their investigation, and she also wanted a chance to talk to Ike.

Especially since Ike might be on the verge of being arrested.

Eden tried not to speculate as to what had happened. Instead, she hurried to the bathroom to get dressed while Rory made his way downstairs. When she joined him less than five minutes later, she found him in the kitchen with Dutton, Grace, Nash, Leslie and Tyler. Tyler was in a high chair and was making a mess with his oatmeal.

"Rory told us," Grace said, and even though she had her baby cuddled in her arms, it was obvious she was champing at the bit to be involved with the case. Thankfully, she didn't insist, though. "Bennie dropped off a cruiser about a half hour ago," she added a moment later.

Rory nodded his thanks and took the keys that Grace motioned to on the table. "We'll let you know the details as soon as we have them," Rory assured her, and then he shifted his attention to Dutton. They didn't say anything to each other, but a look passed between them.

A look of dread, mixed with relief.

Because if Ike was indeed the killer, they could arrest him so he couldn't harm anyone else. But it wouldn't be easy for them to grasp that their father had tried to kill his own son.

Dutton handed them to-go cups of coffee and two wrapped breakfast sandwiches. Eden took them, knowing she'd need the coffee but no way would she risk eating with her stomach churning the way it was.

However, Rory did start eating one as soon as they were in the cruiser. Maybe because he knew this was going to turn into a hellishly long day and that he'd need the fuel.

They drove away from the ranch and toward the sign that was only a couple of miles away. Unfortunately, it wasn't near any houses or businesses, so there probably wouldn't be any eyewitnesses. Still, they might be able to get some sort of confession from Ike or info from someone who'd driven past and saw something suspicious going on.

They were still about a half mile from the sign when Rory got a text, and the message from Detective Vernon appeared on the dash.

Search warrant executed. CSIs are going through Diedre Bennington's home, office and vehicle. She's not at her residence, but a housekeeper let us in.

Where is she? Rory texted back.

Apparently, at the gym. She's on her way to the house now. Will let you know if anything turns up.

Rory sent him back a thanks and glanced at her. "I'll fill him in, too, on Carter's death once we know what's going on."

Yes, because SAPD would need to get involved in that as well since Carter lived in San Antonio.

The moment the sign came into view, Eden saw that the deputies had already blocked off both lanes and put up a detour sign, which would basically mean any through traffic would have to do a U-turn and find another route. She also saw their cruiser parked behind Ike's truck, which was on the narrow shoulder of the road. Ike was sitting on the tailgate, and he was staring at the body.

It was Carter, all right.

The man had been propped up against one of the posts that held the sign, and his head had lolled to one side. Even before she got out of the cruiser and went closer, Eden could see the blood all over his shirt.

Rory parked the cruiser, and they fired glances around them as they made their way to Garrison, who was already walking toward them. Judson was next to Ike, and it was obvious the deputy was guarding him even though Ike's hands hadn't been restrained. Restraints were the protocol if a suspect was aggressive or likely to attempt escape, but apparently, Judson and Garrison hadn't felt the need for such measures.

"I didn't touch him, and the ME and CSIs are on the way, but I'm certain he was stabbed and bled out," Garrison told them right off.

Like Mellie and Brenda. And they had also been left in a sitting position at the barn. Since the barn no longer existed, the killer must have chosen this spot for the dump.

But, no...

Eden quickly amended that thought when she went

closer and saw the blood. Carter hadn't been dumped here. He'd been killed here.

"I'm pretty sure those are stun-gun marks on his neck," Garrison went on while all three of them studied the body.

Eden didn't go closer because she didn't want to destroy any potential evidence, but she leaned in enough to spot the marks on his neck. Yes, a stun gun.

"Has he confessed to killing Carter?" Rory asked, tipping his head to Ike, who wasn't being his usual boisterous, obnoxious self. In fact, he seemed to be in shock.

Garrison shook his head. "Nope. Just the opposite. He said someone called him to come here if he wanted to save a person from dying." His tone let them know that he wasn't buying it.

But Eden was.

Sort of.

"I don't see any blood on Ike," Eden muttered. "Was there anything in his truck? Bloody clothes? Or cleaning supplies?"

"None that I found," Garrison admitted. "I checked the truck, and there was a handgun in the glove compartment. I took that into custody, and it's locked up in the back of the cruiser. I got his phone, too, since I figured we'd need to check to see if he did get a call."

He held up the plastic evidence bag he was holding with the cell inside it, and he passed it to Eden when she motioned for it.

"Ike gave me the password to unlock the phone," Garrison went on, "and there was a call from an unknown number about thirty minutes ago."

So Ike could have been telling the truth about that. Or else this was a situation like Brenda's, with the burner sending the replies being found in her home.

"And did you find a knife on Ike or in the truck?" Eden persisted.

"No," the deputy answered. "There was a tire iron, but nothing I can see that would have been used to make those stab wounds. There are a lot of them," he murmured. "This was overkill."

Yes, it was. It was hard to tell with all the blood now soaking the dead man's clothes, but Eden could see at least five cut marks in his shirt. Then, there were the two on his neck. Those would have likely been fatal if one of the others hadn't killed him.

Eden continued to look at the body. "Rigor hasn't completely set in Carter, so he probably hasn't been dead more than a couple of hours. Added to that, if he'd been out here for long, someone would have likely spotted him."

Yes, it was early, but this was ranching country, where some started their day before sunrise.

The killer sure had.

Because if Carter had been at his home in San Antonio, the killer would have had to somehow snatch him, bring him here and murder him. After that, the body would have been posed.

All without someone seeing what was going on.

"There appears to be arterial spray," Rory commented, motioning toward the spatter on the signpost and the grass around the body. "Blood would have gotten on the killer."

Garrison lifted his shoulder. "I guess Ike couldn't have gone home and changed, or he could have been wearing some kind of protective gear. Or another possibility is that he stashed the clothes, and they're around here somewhere." But he stopped, and his forehead bunched up.

Obviously, the deputy had seen the problem with those theories. Why would Ike have murdered Carter, then left the scene, changed his clothes and returned? And if he'd had on protective gear to prevent being spattered with blood, where was it? Yes, he could have hidden it nearby, but why not just leave once he'd killed Carter?

However, Eden did think of one possible scenario that would fit what she was seeing here. "It's possible Ike came back to retrieve some kind of evidence," she muttered. "Maybe something he dropped. But that would be a huge risk."

Rory made a sound of agreement. "And if he had left something behind and found it, he could have said someone had put it there to set him up." He glanced at Garrison. "Any chance of tracing the anonymous call that reported the location of the body?"

"None," Garrison grumbled. "I checked that on the way over here, and it was a burner."

Of course, it was, but it would be interesting to hear what Ike had to say about who'd called him to the scene.

"We'll talk to him," Rory said as if reading Eden's thoughts, "but we'll move into the cruiser for that. Be careful," he added to Garrison. "If someone is setting up Ike, that someone could still be around. And there could be explosives, so go ahead and get the bomb squad out here to do a sweep before anyone starts checking the scene. Oh, and have the bomb squad check the body, too."

Garrison's eyes widened, and he muttered a single word of profanity. "You think there could be explosives underneath the body?"

"It's possible they could be anywhere out here," Rory explained.

The deputy made some glances around them, and his nerves were definitely showing. There were thick woods here, like more of the area outside of town, but there were a few trees surrounded by tall grass.

It was the perfect place to plant an IED.

Of course, if the killer still wanted Rory and her dead, this would be a good opportunity to use a sniper to gun them down. That was obviously a pressing concern for Rory because he didn't take any more time with Garrison, and they went straight to Ike and Judson.

"Garrison will fill you in on potential problems," Rory told Judson, and he hiked his thumb in the direction of the cruiser. "You're coming with us," he added to Ike.

Eden expected Ike to balk. He didn't. For once, Ike didn't lash out with any of his usual venomous remarks. With his gaze seemingly frozen on the dead man, he just got off the tailgate and followed them to the cruiser. Ike was placed in the back seat, and they took the front.

This wasn't an ideal place for questioning a murder suspect, but as acting sheriff, Rory should stay on the scene until at least some of the other responders arrived. After that, they could take Ike to the police station, where he'd need to be formally interviewed by someone other than Rory or her.

"I know Livvy read you your rights yesterday," Rory began, "but let me repeat it." And that's what he did.

Again, Ike didn't lash out. Didn't demand a lawyer. But he did ask a question the moment Rory had finished with the Miranda warning.

"Who is he?" Ike still had that frozen look of shock in his eyes.

"You don't know?" Rory countered.

That seemed to snap Ike out of his trance, and his gaze fired to Rory. "I wouldn't have asked if I already knew. Who the hell is he?"

Rory stared at his father a long time as if trying to suss out if this was an act. "Carter Rooney."

Eden carefully watched Ike's face for signs of recognition, but she didn't see any. Just the opposite. If Ike was faking all of this, then he was doing a stellar job of it.

Ike repeated the dead man's name a couple of times as if trying to jog his memory, and then he shook his head. "I don't know him," he concluded.

She and Rory exchanged a glance before he continued. "So how did you end up here at the crime scene of someone you didn't even know?"

"I got a call," Ike said after a long pause. "I don't know who from. It said 'unknown caller' on the screen, but I answered it, anyway. Sometimes, it's a horse seller who isn't in my contacts. Anyway, the person was whispering, like they were trying to disguise their voice, and he said if I wanted to stop Tyler from dying that I'd get here to the sign fast and save him."

Every muscle in Eden's body tightened. "Tyler," she blurted.

The panic came, roaring through her, and then she felt Rory take hold of her hand and give it a gentle squeeze. "Tyler's safe," he reminded her. "Grace and Dutton won't let anyone get near him."

She mentally replayed every word of that until it finally sank in. Their baby was all right. Using Tyler's name had merely been a threat. Still, it was going to take a while for her nerves to settle.

"Of course, I had to come," Ike went on several moments later. "I mean, he's my grandson no matter what's gone on between the three of us."

That wasn't exactly an outpouring of grandfatherly love, but Eden believed his concern for Tyler was the real deal.

And Ike had come here even though he must have known there was a possibility he'd be facing down a killer. That didn't erase the ugliness that'd gone on between them, but Eden would always be thankful for his response.

Well, if Ike was telling the full truth, that was.

"Why didn't you call the police station? Or us when you got a call like that?" Rory asked.

"Because the caller said if I did, then I'd never see Tyler alive again." He stopped and cursed. The words were vicious and filled with rage. "That SOB was going to hurt a baby because of me. I couldn't let that happen," he muttered. "I had to hurry here and try to save him."

"What did you see when you got here?" Rory continued after a long pause. Hearing that about Tyler had likely shaken him, too.

"Not Tyler, that's for sure. Or the two of you." Ike paused. "I thought maybe...well, I thought the killer had taken both of you, too."

So he'd expected to find all of them being held hostage. Or already dead. Again, that was the case if he was telling the truth, and Eden hadn't heard anything from him yet that felt like a flat-out lie.

"I drove up to the sign and stopped when I saw the body," Ike added to his explanation.

"Did you touch the body or anything around it?" Rory asked quickly.

"No, hell, no. I could see he was dead. Blood everywhere. And his eyes." He didn't shudder, but it was a similar reaction. "There was no life in those eyes."

Again, Eden had to agree. Even from the distance of Ike's truck to the body, she would have realized Carter was dead. No movement. All that blood, and his eyes had been wide open.

"I looked around," Ike added, "but I didn't see anyone. And then the two deputies came barreling up. That's when I knew I'd been framed." He looked at Rory. "I don't expect you to believe that, but it's the truth, and that means you don't have a killer here in this cruiser. He or she is out there, ready to strike again until I'm locked up for murder."

"Who would do that?" Rory asked.

"Helen or Diedre," Ike said without any hesitation. "Hell, they could be working together."

That was indeed possible since the women had been together at Diedre's house.

"And, no, I don't have any proof that one or both is behind this," Ike went on. "But Helen sure as hell could have gotten access to my house to plant those bugs."

True, but Diedre could have as well, if she'd hired someone to break in. Normally, the ranch wasn't as secure as it was now, and the gate was often left open for deliveries and such.

Eden looked up when she heard the sound of an approaching engine, and she silently cursed the flashback that she got of the collision and explosion the day before. It was going to be a while, if ever, before those images left her, but she shoved them aside and saw both CSI and ME vans pull to a stop behind the other cruiser.

"I'll be right back," Rory said, and stepped out. But then he leaned down and gave Ike a warning glance through the metal grating before he started toward the responders.

Since the back doors couldn't open from the inside, Eden wasn't worried about Ike trying to escape. The man wasn't stupid, and he would know something like that would lead to an immediate takedown and arrest.

"I wouldn't try to kill either of you." Ike's grumble was

barely audible. "What happens now?" he asked, loud enough for her to hear.

Eden tried to keep her cop's voice in place despite feeling so darn shaky. "We go back to the station, where you'll be processed. We'll need your clothes for testing, and Livvy will have some questions for you."

"Right." And the sarcasm and snark had returned. "No more questions until my lawyers are there. I'm not saying another damn word that could get me in even hotter water than I already am."

So some of the old Ike had returned, but she couldn't blame him for lawyering up again. If there was any physical evidence linking him to this murder, then he would almost certainly be arrested.

Since Ike had clammed up, Eden used her phone to text Detective Vernon to ask him to check on the alibis for Helen and Diedre. Even if they had them, the women would need to be brought in for another round of interviews.

Eden tried not to be frustrated that the investigation seemed to be going in circles. Three murders, and they still hadn't managed to positively ID or arrest the killer. With her and Rory's names on that hit list, the pressure was skyrocketing for them to put a stop to this, especially since the killer knew about Tyler.

Rory returned to the cruiser, and he slid in behind the wheel, automatically studying her face. No doubt to see if Ike had said anything in his absence.

"Ike wants his lawyers," Eden informed him.

Rory huffed but didn't seem surprised. Nor did he discuss the murder. Probably because Ike would have been able to hear every word. He just started the cruiser, then drove past the other responders and straight into town. It took them less than two minutes to reach the police station, a reminder of just how bold the killer had been to leave Carter's body practically right on their doorstep.

They led Ike inside, where Livvy was already waiting for them. "His phone's been taken into evidence," Rory informed her. "So he'll need to use the landline to contact his lawyers."

Livvy nodded and volleyed glances at the three of them. She was probably trying to figure out what the heck was going on. Sadly, Eden and Rory were doing the same thing.

"I can let him use the phone on my desk," Livvy said. "And then I can take him to interview room one. Do you also want me to get the contact info for the victim's next of kin so they can be notified?"

"Yes, do that. And thanks," Rory told her.

Livvy tipped her head toward Grace's office. "You two have a visitor, and he's insisting on talking to you."

Eden looked in that direction and saw Frank Mott. So, apparently, he had surfaced after all. Since the man hadn't returned their calls and no one had seen or heard from him, Eden had thought he might have met the same fate as Carter.

Frank came to the doorway of Grace's office, doling out a scowl to Ike. And Ike scowled right back.

"Are you the one setting me up?" Ike snarled.

Frank lifted his shoulder as if the question had been about something mundane rather than about murder.

"Frank," Rory greeted as they went into the office. "We've been trying to contact you."

The man nodded. "Yes, I was out at my fishing cabin on the lake. No cell service. I didn't get your messages until I got home late last night. I figured rather than call you so late, I'd just come and see you face-to-face." He paused. "Did Ike kill that man?"

"How did you know someone was dead?" Rory countered.

Frank shrugged. "Hard not to hear something like that. The two deputies were hurrying to the scene when I got here. Why did you want to talk to me?" he quickly added, and Eden didn't think it was her imagination that he was trying to curtail any more discussion as to how he'd learned about Carter's death.

Rory gave him a long, hard look before he went to a laptop on the desk and he pulled up the photos that Carter had given them. The lab had already enhanced them so that the images were much clearer now. Rory pulled up the shot of Frank and turned the laptop so the man could see the screen.

"What? Where was that taken...?" But Frank's voice trailed off when he must have recognized the surroundings. "Who took that photo?" he demanded.

Rory didn't give him the answer. "Want to explain to me why you were there and what you were doing?"

A flash of panic went through his eyes. "Am I under arrest? Do you think I killed that man?" He didn't wait for Rory to respond. "Because I didn't. I thought you were trying to get in touch with me about something else..." Again, his words slowed to a crawl, and he squeezed his eyes shut a moment.

"What's the *something else* you thought I'd want to know?" Rory demanded, and he was all cop now. Then, he held up his hand. "Let me go ahead and read you your Miranda rights."

Frank shook his head as if not believing this was happening, but he didn't speak when Rory read him his rights. Nor did he lawyer up at the end of it.

"I didn't kill anyone," Frank blurted the moment Rory

had finished. He motioned toward the photo still on the screen. "And I was there because, uh, I've been seeing Diedre."

"Seeing?" Rory queried.

Frank swallowed hard. "I'm in a relationship with her. Or at least I was, but she broke it off a couple of days ago."

Interesting. "Before or after Brenda's murder?" Eden asked.

"Before," Frank muttered. "I didn't want things to end between us so I drove to her place to talk to her, but I parked and watched the house for a little while so I could see if she was alone. Helen is there sometimes."

Eden was sure she had a puzzled look in her eyes. Rory had one as well. "Explain that," Rory insisted.

Frank certainly didn't jump right on that. He took a couple of moments and groaned under his breath, as if this wasn't something he wanted to spill. "Diedre wanted to keep our relationship a secret."

Again, Eden was puzzled. "Why?" she persisted. "You're both single, aren't you?"

"We are, but then there's Helen." Frank's groan turned to a loud huff. "Helen and I saw each other for a while—"

"Wait," Eden interrupted. "You told us you hadn't been romantically involved with Helen."

"I told you we hadn't been when I was a teenager," Frank snapped out. "Back then, I was seeing Mellie. And, no, I didn't bring that up when she was killed because it was a hell of a long time ago."

Eden folded her arms over her chest. "You didn't think it was pertinent to tell us that you had a romantic history with a woman who was murdered in the very barn where you two used to work?"

"No." He stopped, scowled. "It wasn't relevant," he insisted. "Mellie and I dated for a couple of months, and we broke up. It was just teenage stuff, definitely nothing serious. I got involved with Miranda shortly thereafter, and Mellie inherited the place she eventually turned into the foster ranch. Mellie and I moved on with our lives."

"And then became enemies," Eden reminded him.

He shot her a stony look. "Yeah, we did, but that was on Mellie. You were raised in that foster home, and you know what some of those kids were always doing to my property. Knocking down fences, letting the livestock out. Hell, even taking some of my horses for joyrides."

All of that had indeed happened, and while Eden didn't believe any serious damage had been done, she could understand why Mellie and Frank had butted heads over the years. Mellie had been trying to raise kids, and Frank had been trying to run his ranch. However, she had to wonder if their past had played into the ferocity of some of the conflicts. Eden recalled plenty of loud arguments between the two and heated threats from Frank.

Frank was obviously experiencing some of that anger now, but he didn't make any threats. He just stood there a few moments as if steadying himself. Eden did the same, and she shifted the conversation back to the original topic.

"Helen," she stated. "When did you get romantically involved with her?"

"Romance," he muttered, as if that wasn't anywhere close to the truth. "We hooked up for the first time right before she left for college. That's continued over the years. Not while I was married. I never cheated on my wife," he insisted. "But a couple of years after she passed away, Helen and I ran into each other, and we...reconnected. We still have what I guess you'd call an open-ended arrangement."

Eden wondered if that was his way of saying friends with benefits.

"Look," Frank went on, shifting his attention to Rory, "Helen has had it in for Diedre since your mom died. And, yes, I understand that, what with Diedre having an affair with her sister's husband, but Helen seems to have finally put that behind her. She's not trying to make Diedre's life miserable."

"Had Helen been doing that?" Eden prompted when the man fell silent.

"Definitely. Helen and Ike were essentially doing the same thing. Dissing Diedre to potential clients, taking every opportunity to badmouth her. It put Diedre under a lot of stress, and I don't want her to have to go back to that kind of relationship with Helen." He stopped and seemed to have a debate about what he was going to say. It took him a couple of moments to continue. "At times, Helen can be very scary."

"Scary?" Rory repeated, and it was very much a question.

"Yes." Another pause. "Last month she asked me about explosives."

That grabbed Eden and Rory's attention. "What specifically did she ask?" Rory asked.

"She wanted to know if I had any experience with them when I was in the military. I didn't. I was a cargo pilot," he explained. "When I pressed her as to why she wanted to know, she said she was considering donating to a foundation that helped veterans injured by IEDs."

Rory kept his intense gaze on Frank. "Did you believe her?"

Frank shrugged, hardly a wholehearted confirmation that he thought she'd told him the truth. "Like I said, Helen can be scary, and that's why I don't want you to mention that I've been seeing Diedre. Don't say anything about it to Ike, either."

Once again, Eden was surprised. "Why not? Why would he care if Diedre had been with you?"

Another shrug from Frank. "I think some of the bad-mouthing that Ike does is because he still has feelings for Diedre. I have no proof of that," Frank said quickly, "but Diedre is a very desirable woman, and she dumped Ike. He'll say it was the other way around, but it wasn't. She dumped him, and he wasn't ready for things to end."

Eden wasn't sure it mattered who'd been the one to break things off. And she didn't believe Ike's venom for the woman was seeded in him still having feelings for her. Of course, it was possible. She just couldn't see that as a motive for the murders.

"You also didn't mention that you knew Brenda," Rory mused.

Frank seemed to freeze for a moment. "I didn't know her. Not really."

"Not really?" Eden repeated and waited to see if he was going to mention Brenda calling him about going to the I-hate-Ike luncheon she'd arranged.

"Not really," he snapped. "The woman was a pest, wanting me to team up with her to take Ike down. I declined. I told her to let karma deal with Ike."

Frank didn't seem like a karma-believing sort of guy. But Eden could see Brenda pressing him to join the group she was assembling. Could see Frank declining, too, especially if he didn't want to be in the same room with Helen and Diedre.

"Did you ever go to Brenda's house?" Rory asked.

"No," Frank responded. "But she dropped by mine once."

I didn't even let her in. So, no, her DNA won't be at my place, and mine won't be at hers. You're barking up the wrong tree, deputies. I have absolutely no motive to kill Mellie or Brenda."

That wasn't true in Mellie's case. Bad blood was often a motive for murder. But Eden couldn't see that bad blood extending to Brenda. Yes, she'd seemingly pressured Frank into joining her anti-Ike group, but turning her down wasn't a reason to kill her.

"I need to go," Frank insisted, checking the time. "I'm meeting someone for breakfast."

"Sorry, but I'm going to need you to make a formal statement about that photo," Rory explained. "Go down the hall to interview room two and wait. I'll be there in a couple of minutes."

Frank glared at both of them for a long time, and for a moment Eden thought the man was going to refuse. He didn't. He stormed off, taking out his phone, maybe to call a lawyer.

Rory didn't add anything else until Frank was out of hearing range. "I can't tell if he just threw Helen under the bus so we'd think she's the killer, or if he's truly worried she could be behind the murders."

"Same," Eden agreed. But either way, Frank was now solidly a suspect.

Rory turned to her. "I can take his statement solo if you want to find out what's going on at the latest crime scene."

She nodded, already coming up with a mental list of things she needed to do. Touching base with the bomb squad was a high priority. But she also wanted to check Frank's military service records to see if he did indeed have the explosives experience that he had denied.

However, Eden had barely made it a step toward her

desk when Rory's phone rang, and she stopped when she heard him say, "It's Detective Vernon."

She turned back into the office, and he answered the call. He didn't put it on speaker, but after just a handful of seconds, Eden knew something was wrong. She prayed there hadn't been yet another murder.

"All right, do that," Rory said to Vernon after a couple of snail-crawling moments—moments that Eden spent on edge. "And have the lab contact me as soon as they know."

He ended the call and looked at her. "The CSIs searching Diedre's house found a Swiss Army knife."

Eden immediately thought of the incident that Dutton had witnessed. The one where Helen had threatened Ike, and he'd snatched the knife from her. That one had been a Swiss Army knife.

"Is it the murder weapon?" she asked, wondering how it'd gotten from Ike to Diedre's.

"Maybe. The lab will have to determine that. There are no prints on it, the handle has been wiped clean, but the CSIs thought they spotted something at the base of the blade, so they did a preliminary test on scene." Rory stopped and gathered his breath. "It tested positive for human blood."

Chapter Twelve

Rory stared at his phone and filled Eden in on the rest of the conversation that he'd just had with the detective. "Vernon volunteered to have one of the uniformed officers who was already on the scene at her house escort Diedre here to Renegade Canyon. I took him up on that. She'll be here soon."

"Good," Eden muttered.

Rory could practically hear Eden making a mental tally of what was on their slate today. Diedre was yet one more thing on their to-do list on what would undoubtedly turn out to be a hellishly long day. A day that had barely gotten started.

But he didn't have an option when it came to talking to Diedre. He had to get her in for an official interrogation not only about the knife, but also because of what Frank had said about them being in a relationship. Along with that, he needed to confirm if Frank had been telling the truth. Because if he'd lied, then that put the guilty spotlight right on the man since he could have planted the knife in Diedre's house.

However, if Diedre was the killer, if she was the one responsible for those three deaths and for Eden and him nearly being killed, then Rory wanted to know so he could lock her up. That could prevent others from being killed.

Including Eden.

She was holding it together, but he could see the strain in her eyes. And the fear. Not for herself but because Tyler was potentially in danger as well. That was the worst kind of pressure for a parent.

Even though the timing sucked, he closed the office door and pulled her to him. He didn't kiss her. Nope. Not nearly enough time for that, but the hug was enough to steady him some. When he eased back from her, he thought it'd done the same for her. They would definitely need steadying because of what they had to do next.

"Did Vernon say if Diedre admitted that the knife was hers?" she asked.

He shook his head. "She insisted someone planted it, that maybe we even did it when we visited her."

Eden sighed. "She's reaching. We weren't out of her sight the whole time we were there at her place." She paused. "But Helen was."

"Yep." His aunt had come into the room while Eden and he had been talking to Diedre, so she would have had free rein of the rest of the house before her entrance. "And we'll need to talk to her today, too."

To get that ball rolling, Rory located his aunt's number in his contacts and called her. Because it was still fairly early, he figured the call might go to voice mail, but she answered right away.

"Are Eden and you all right?" Helen asked, but there was no real concern, or even interest, in her voice. It seemed more like something she should say rather than something she especially wanted to know. "I heard there was another murder."

Rory didn't bother to huff. Yeah, bad news was definitely traveling fast. "We weren't hurt," he simply said, since they were far from all right. "But I need to talk to you."

"About what?" she asked after a long pause.

"Some questions have come up, and I want to discuss a couple of things with you." Rory made sure he used his cop's tone so she'd know this was all business. "How soon can you come to the police station?"

He heard Helen take in a long breath. "I can be there in about ten minutes. I'm in Renegade Canyon," she added. Judging from the background, he thought she was in her car.

Now, it was his turn to pause. "Were you visiting your friend in the hospital, the one who had an appendectomy?" Rory asked. "What was her name again?" he added.

"Sheila Mendoza," Helen informed him without hesitation. "But, no, I wasn't visiting her. I'm on the way to the cemetery to put flowers on my sister's grave. She's been on my mind a lot lately, and I brought her some roses."

Rory knew that Helen had done that in the past, but he didn't like the timing of this visit. Then again, with Ike being front and center in the investigation, his mother had been on Rory's mind, too. So maybe Helen was telling the truth.

Maybe.

"I'll be at the police station soon," Helen assured him and ended the call.

Rory didn't put his phone away, though. He accessed the database that had contact info for most people in town, and he located the number he was looking for.

"You're calling Sheila Mendoza," Eden murmured after

glancing at what he was doing. She moved closer, so she'd be able to hear.

"Yep. I want to hear what she has to say..." He had to stop when Sheila answered on the first ring.

Since he didn't know the woman that well, Rory made the greeting more formal. "Mrs. Mendoza, this is Deputy Rory McClennan."

"Rory," she said, sounding a whole lot friendlier than Helen had been. "I didn't expect to hear from someone in the police station. Is everything all right?"

Maybe there was someone who hadn't heard about the murder after all. "I just want to verify something. Are you still in the hospital?"

"Oh, no. I'm home. I just had that one night's stay. Nothing serious. Why?" she asked.

Rory evaded the question and jumped straight to the reason for the call. "Did my Aunt Helen visit you while you were still in the hospital?"

"Yes, she did," Sheila confirmed. "That was so sweet of her."

So Helen was telling the truth. That nixed his theory that Helen had murdered Brenda and then shown up at the hospital only to give herself a possible alibi if someone had indeed spotted her near or in town.

"A sweet surprise," Sheila went on.

"A surprise, how?" Rory persisted.

"Well, I mean because I didn't know she was coming. And we're not exactly friends. Don't get me wrong," she continued, "she's always been friendly enough to me, but I hadn't actually talked to her since your mom's funeral, and that was just to say hello and how sorry I was. It was so kind of her to think of visiting me on a trip to town."

"She didn't mention if visiting you was the main reason for her trip?" Rory queried.

"Golly, I don't think so. She just showed up, and we chatted for a while before she left."

Rory had to put a mental question mark by his earlier conclusion of Helen telling the truth. The visit could have still been to cover up her presence in town.

"Was there, uh, anything unusual about Helen during that visit?" Rory went on. "I mean, did she seem upset or nervous? How did she look?"

He wasn't surprised when the woman didn't answer right away. She was no doubt wondering what this was all about. "I guess she seemed fine. She looked all right, too. What happened? What's wrong? Did something happen to Helen?"

"Helen is okay," he assured her. "I'm just trying to pinpoint a lot of different people's movements that night, and you've helped with that. Thank you."

He wrapped up the call with Sheila and then immediately groaned. "I should have found an excuse to have Helen's clothes and hands tested for blood when we saw her in the hospital."

Eden rolled her eyes. "There would have been no legal excuse for that. Helen wasn't even a suspect at the time."

"No, but she should have been. I should have had her on the suspect list right from the start, because of her extreme hatred for Ike. My mother's death could have been the trigger that set all of these murders in motion."

"Maybe, but why not just go after Ike?" Eden asked, clearly playing devil's advocate.

"Having him rot in jail would be a lot more punishment," Rory replied.

Of course, that didn't explain why Helen hadn't just

gone after Diedre first since Diedre had caused Rory's mom so much pain by having an affair with Ike.

Unless...

"Maybe Helen is planning on setting up Diedre for the murders, too," he muttered. "That way, she could maybe get both Diedre and Ike behind bars."

Eden didn't disagree this time, and he could see her processing that theory. It had plenty of merit, but obviously there were some pieces that didn't fit, and Eden voiced one of them.

"Why kill Carter?" she asked.

Rory had to shrug. "The man liked to take pictures, so maybe Helen thought he'd taken an incriminating one of her. Or one that would inadvertently give Diedre an alibi that Helen wouldn't want her to have."

Again, Eden didn't disagree, but she also didn't have a chance to dole out any more potential questions because they heard the voices in the squad room and turned in that direction. It was Ike's legal team, and Stephen Arnette was making a beeline toward them. Judging from his irate expression and body language, Rory figured he knew what the lawyer was about to say.

"I demand that my client be immediately released," Arnette snarled.

Yep, that's exactly what Rory figured Arnette would demand. "It's not happening. Your client was found at the scene with someone who'd been murdered. At minimum, he needs to be questioned and give a statement."

Arnette's eyes narrowed. "Is he under arrest?"

"Not at the moment, but it's a possibility," Rory admitted. He didn't add more because he saw Helen come in. "Your client is in interview room one," he said, and he stepped around the team to head toward Helen.

Helen's eyes weren't narrowed, not yet, anyway, but her hard expression made it clear she wasn't happy to be here.

"This way," Rory said, leading her toward Grace's office. Thankfully, the lawyers were already on their way to interview so Rory didn't have to deal with them.

Once he had Helen inside the office, he closed the door and motioned for her to take a seat next to the desk. Eden took the one next to her, causing Helen to flick her a glance that seemed to be tinged with annoyance. He wasn't positive what Helen's beef was with Eden, but he suspected it was because Eden was the mother of his child. Any association with him would spur Helen's disapproval, since his aunt blamed him for not doing more to save his mother's life.

"Do you need me to go over your Miranda rights again?" Rory asked, leaning his hip against the edge of the desk.

"No. I haven't suddenly developed amnesia," she said. "Just ask your questions, and if I decide I want my lawyer here, I'll call him. But please be quick. Your mother's flowers are still in my car, and I don't want them to wilt."

He didn't bother to point out that they'd soon wilt in this heat. Or remind her that his mom hadn't actually been a flower lover because of her allergies. No need to dive into the petty stuff since he had bigger fish to fry.

"What's this about?" Helen demanded.

"The knife. Your knife," he amended. "The one you pulled on Ike during the middle of an argument."

She huffed. "I already explained that I didn't *pull* it on him. That makes it sound as if I planned on attacking him. I didn't. I simply wanted to scare him. It didn't work. He ripped the knife from my hand and took it." Helen leaned forward in the chair, pinning her gaze on Rory. "And once again, I have to know if Ike is using that knife to set me up. Did he use it to kill Brenda and that dead man you found earlier?"

Rory went with a similar response to the one he'd given her at Diedre's. "No proof of that. But I do have proof that Ike had the knife returned to you."

That was close to the truth, anyway. The photo Ike's assistant had taken showed something in an envelope being left on Helen's doorstep.

Helen stared at him and shook her head. "He didn't, and if Ike said he did, he's lying."

"Proof," Rory repeated. "The knife was left at your house."

Helen shook her head again. "No, it wasn't. Or if it was, I never received it." Her denial seemed genuine.

Seemed.

"If the knife was left at my house, then it was stolen," Helen went on. "Or else Ike faked sending it. I'll say it again—Ike will use that knife to try to set me up. Or murder me with it. Why haven't you arrested him?"

"Because I need proof for that," Rory said, honestly. "And so far, it looks more as if someone is setting up Ike, not you."

If looks could kill, Helen would have ended him right then, right there. "Are you accusing me of murder?"

"Not accusing. Asking," he clarified. "Did you kill Mellie and Brenda?" He didn't add Carter's name since the man's family hadn't been notified yet.

"No, I did not," she snapped, and she stood. "And if that's all you want—"

"It's not," Rory said, stepping in front of her to block her from leaving. "Have you had any recent conversations with anyone about explosives?"

For just a second, Helen got that deer-caught-in-the-headlights look, but she quickly reined in her shock. "Why do you ask?"

"Just answer the question," he insisted.

She took her time doing that. "Frank Mott. He told you I was asking about that." Helen waved a dismissive hand. "I certainly didn't want to know so I could blow something up." She paused again. "I was trying to make a connection with him, all right?"

Rory was sure he looked confused, because he was. "Excuse me?"

Not shock this time from Helen, but what he thought was embarrassment. "A connection. I wanted to talk about something that I thought would interest him since he has all these guns and military magazines around his house. Frank and I have been seeing each other, but he seemed to be losing interest so I wanted to...connect," she explained.

Rory wasn't sure he bought that, but he would now need to ask Frank about those magazines. They might turn out to be nothing, but since the killer had used IEDs twice now, that was definitely an angle that needed to be investigated.

"Would you agree to having your home searched?" Rory asked her.

Muscles stirred and tightened in Helen's jaw. "And what exactly would you hope to find in such a search?" But she didn't wait for an answer. She began to snap out the possibilities. "A knife that I've already told you I don't have? Clothes with Brenda's and Mellie's blood on them? A printed-out confession of crimes I didn't do? Or maybe you'll actually find something that Ike planted to try to get back at me. How about all of the above?"

Rory ignored her sarcasm, but if she was innocent she shouldn't have anything to hide. Well, unless she was truly worried that something had been planted. If so, they needed to find whatever that was and try to sort everything out.

"If you don't agree to a search, I could request a warrant," Rory told her.

Helen didn't react. She just seemed to hold her ground, though he figured there was a firestorm of anger boiling inside her.

"Get the warrant," she growled. "And I truly hope your mother isn't watching you right now from her grave because she'd be sick at what her son is trying to do to her only sister."

Rory had a comeback for that. "She'd be even sicker if her sister didn't cooperate with a murder investigation that could save lives. Maybe even Eden's and mine."

Helen opened her mouth to say something, but with her jaw clenched, she was going to have trouble speaking. Maybe that's why she didn't add anything else for several long moments.

"Is there something else you want to badger me with, or am I free to leave this witch hunt?" Helen demanded.

Rory glanced at Eden to see if she had any other questions, and when she shook her head, he gave Helen a nod. She didn't waste a second throwing open the door and heading out.

And nearly ran into Diedre.

The two women seemed to startle each other, and then they both stood there for a couple of seconds as if waiting for the other to speak.

"Your turn in the box," Helen finally muttered before she walked away.

Part of Rory wanted to go after his aunt because, after all, she was his mother's sister. But he had no idea what to say to her. He certainly couldn't assure her that everything would be all right because there was a killer still at large.

And that killer could be Helen.

However, if it turned out not to be her, then he was going to owe her an apology when this was all over. But for now, he had to do his job, and part of that job was turning over every stone to stop a killer from striking again.

"You didn't say anything to Helen about Frank and me, did you?" Diedre whispered, casting an uneasy glance at Helen from over her shoulder.

Rory was about to answer and let her know that he hadn't, but he saw Livvy making her way to him, so he and Eden stepped out of the office to see what Livvy wanted.

"Wait in the office," Rory told Diedre. "We won't be long."

Livvy waited until Diedre was out of earshot before she spoke. "The ME just called," Livvy whispered, "and he used facial recognition to confirm that the body is Carter Rooney."

Not a surprise since both he and Eden had recognized him, but the official confirmation from the ME was a necessary step in this process.

"Did the ME find anything else?" Rory asked.

Livvy shook her head. "Not yet. He hasn't actually examined the body yet. The bomb squad just arrived, and they're checking the area first. Once it's clear, he'll go in and do his initial assessment before the body is taken to the morgue for a postmortem."

Good. Rory didn't want any of the responders at risk because of other IEDs. Which made him think of something Helen had said.

"See if Bennie has the time to do some more digging into Frank's background," Rory said. "Helen told us that he was into explosives, and I'd like to know if that's true. And if so, just how into it is he. I need to know if Frank has the expertise to have made those explosive devices."

Again, Livvy nodded. "You also want me to try to get a search warrant for Frank's house?"

Rory thought of the workload that was already on Livvy since she'd be the one who had to deal with Ike. "Have Bennie do that, too. And we need to try to get a search warrant for Helen's house."

Livvy sighed. Not because she was shocked by the news. She was aware Helen was a suspect. But the sigh was no doubt because the woman was his aunt, and that meant two of his family members were suspects in a triple murder.

"I'll let Bennie know," Livvy assured him, and then she showed him the sticky note she was holding. It had the names and contact number for Reva and Harry Rooney. "They're Carter's parents, but they live in Tucson."

Part of Rory was relieved that he wouldn't have to be doing a death notification, but it also meant losing out on the opportunity to ask the couple questions about their son. Still, he figured the Tucson cops would be doing that and passing along any info they got from the parents.

Rory took the sticky note. "When we're done talking to Diedre, I'll call Tucson PD and ask that someone there go out to speak with the Rooneys. Maybe by then, we'll have a bit more from the ME that I can pass along."

"All right. Let me touch base with Bennie on getting those warrants and doing the research on Frank," Livvy said, checking the time, "and then I'll go in and see if Ike is ready to give a statement. Anything specific you want me to press him on?"

Rory considered that a moment and shook his head. "His lawyers will keep him on a tight leash so he doesn't say anything incriminating. Or rather, more incriminating since he was found at the scene with a dead body."

Livvy made a sound of agreement. "I'll press about that phone call he got," she replied. "He might remember something that can help her ID whoever it was that called him."

"Good luck," Rory told her. "As soon as we're done interviewing Diedre, we'll try to observe the rest of the interview with Ike."

Livvy glanced in the direction of Grace's office. "Will you be arresting Diedre?" she asked.

"It's possible. The knife was found in her house, but we have no confirmation yet that it was actually the murder weapon."

But there was the human blood that'd been found on it. That and the fact the knife was technically in her possession were enough to make an arrest. Rory wanted more, though. Hell, he wanted a confession so he could put an end to this nightmare.

Since Rory wanted to do this by the book, he stepped back into the office and motioned for Diedre to follow him. "We'll talk in interview room three," he insisted. "This way."

Diedre did follow Eden and him, but she also glanced back over her shoulder. "Is Helen gone?"

Rory frowned and found it strange that Diedre seemed to be more concerned about Helen than she was an interview with the cops about a murder investigation. Still, Rory didn't question her about that. He led Diedre into interview, and he started the recording. After he'd recited the time, date and the names of those present, he repeated the Miranda warning to Diedre.

"Did you tell Helen about me seeing Frank?" Diedre asked the moment Rory had finished.

Again, he was puzzled by both the woman's reaction and why she would be asking that particular question. But since she'd brought up the subject, he decided to go with it for now.

"You're in a relationship with Frank Mott?" Rory asked.

She huffed. "You know I am. Frank told you, and he called me when the officer was driving me here."

"What exactly did Frank say?" Because Rory needed to know if Frank had coached Diedre about the info she was telling them.

Annoyance, and concern, put some steel in the muscles of her jaw, and she was also nibbling on her bottom lip. "I don't remember his exact words, but he said he'd confessed to seeing me. We don't want Helen to know."

"And why is that?" Eden asked.

The annoyance went up a notch. "Because Helen can be a spiteful woman, and she'd try to get back at Frank and me. You know she would," Diedre insisted. "And I don't want to get on her bad side again."

Yes, Rory did indeed know that Helen could be spiteful, but he figured Diedre would always be on his aunt's bad side. Helen was playing nice with Diedre now for the sake of getting back at Ike, but that didn't mean Helen was finished with hating the woman who was her dead sister's rival.

"You have to promise you won't tell Helen about Frank and me," Diedre added a moment later.

Rory looked her straight in the eyes. "This is a murder investigation," he said coldly. "And I can't promise what info will or won't be divulged."

Alarm shot through Diedre's eyes. "But Helen might kill me if she finds out."

"Kill you for sleeping with a man she had a casual relationship with?" Rory said, lacing his question with some obvious skepticism.

Diedre looked ready to blurt something out, but then she seemed to rethink her response. Rory didn't give her much time before he fired off another question.

"Did Helen kill Mellie, Brenda and Carter? Is that why you're afraid she'll murder you, too?"

Diedre didn't jump to answer, but that alarm was still there. Rory had no idea if it was fake or real. And if it was warranted. Diedre could be reacting this way simply to make them more suspicious of Helen.

"Have you ever seen Helen be violent toward anyone or anything?" Eden said.

"Well, no," Diedre admitted after a long pause. "But she did pull that knife on Ike, and because of my affair with Ike, she already has a reason to hate me. I just don't want her coming after Frank and me."

Rory took a moment to process that. "Does anyone else know about your relationship with Frank?"

Diedre did more chewing on her lip. "I told Mellie. And then a few months later, I told Brenda," she finally admitted.

Well, hell. That was either a seriously bad coincidence or a motive for murder, since both women were now dead. But an affair between two consenting adults couldn't spur a murdering spree.

Could it?

If so, how did Carter fit into it?

When Carter had been in Diedre's neighborhood, she had said she didn't know him. And maybe she didn't. It was possible Carter had photographed something that he shouldn't have. Like Frank and Diedre together. But Rory still couldn't wrap his head around that being the motive for these murders.

To test those waters, though, Rory took out his phone and pulled up a photo of Carter to show Diedre. "Tell me about this man."

Her forehead creased as she studied the picture. "It's that guy who was near my house. Who is he?" The question might or might not have been genuine.

Rory didn't give her the name since the next of kin likely hadn't been notified yet. "He was murdered this morning."

Diedre's eyes widened. "That's the dead man Frank mentioned." She made a gasping sound. "You think Ike killed him?"

"Someone did," Rory answered, and it put a knot in his gut to realize he could be seated across from the actual killer.

He let Diedre stew in the silence for a couple of moments while he kept his hard stare on her. She showed no signs of breaking. Then again, she had to be a tough woman to have ever gotten involved with Ike.

Rory decided to shift the conversation in a different direction. "Tell me about the knife that the CSIs found in your house."

This time, Diedre didn't hesitate. "It's not mine, and I have no idea how it got there. Someone must have tried to frame me with it."

Nothing about that response surprised him, but Rory kept pushing. "I know that Helen has been to your house. What about Frank or Brenda?"

Diedre nodded. "Yes, both have been there..." Her voice trailed off, and she started shaking her head. "You can't think Frank would have left the knife there. He wouldn't," she insisted. "He just wouldn't."

"Maybe," Rory muttered. "What about Brenda? Could she have left it?"

She shook her head, but there was a lot less resolve in her expression this time. "Why would she? And if it's the murder weapon, then it would have been used on her, right? She couldn't have been the one to leave it."

Rory went with another *maybe*, but it was silent this time. They had no idea if Mellie and Brenda had been killed with the same weapon. But he had a problem believing Brenda would have murdered Mellie, tried to frame Diedre and then had been murdered herself. If so, that meant there were two killers.

Brenda. And the one who'd ended her life.

Rory was still considering that possibility when his phone rang, and when he saw Garrison's name on the screen, he knew he had to take the call from the deputy.

"Interview paused," Rory said for the recording. "Deputies McClennan and Gallagher exiting the room." He and Eden stepped out into the hall before he answered and put the call on speaker.

"Rory," Garrison said the moment he was on the line. "The bomb squad cleared the immediate area around the body, and the ME was able to start his exam. There's a message of sorts on the dead guy."

"What kind of message?" Rory asked.

"We're not sure. It's numbers. The ME found it beneath the bloody shirt. And it's not a note," Garrison said, the strain obvious in his voice. "It was, uh, cut into his body. I think you and Eden need to see it."

Chapter Thirteen

Eden kept watch around their surroundings as Rory and she drove away from the police station and back to the crime scene. Rory was darting glances around, too. Because both of them were aware that a trip to, well, to pretty much anywhere could result in another attempt to kill them. Still, this "message" was something they wanted to see.

Numbers that'd been carved into Carter's body.

After hearing that bit of detail from Garrison, they'd quickly postponed the interview with Frank and wrapped up the one with Diedre. While there was some circumstantial evidence against her, it hadn't been enough for them to hold her. Eden suspected the same would be true for Ike, though if any of the four—Diedre, Helen, Frank or Ike—would be arrested today, Ike would likely be the one.

But an arrest was nowhere close to getting a conviction.

There were huge holes in the case against Ike. So either Ike had put those holes in place to assure a nonguilty verdict or he wasn't the killer.

Eden was going with the second option on this. As much as she and Ike despised each other, she just couldn't see him going about getting revenge this way. Too risky. Too cat-and-mouse. She figured if Ike turned killer, then the bodies would have never been discovered, much less placed where they'd be found.

Once they reached the crime scene, Rory pulled to a stop behind the line of vehicles. The other deputies' cruiser, Ike's truck, and the three vans from the ME, CSIs and the bomb squad. The road was still blocked off in both directions and would likely remain that way for most of the day.

Eden spotted two members of the bomb squad using a small robotic device to scan an area about ten yards behind the welcome sign. While they worked, the CSIs were searching the immediate area around the body.

Along with Dewey Galway, the ME, their two fellow deputies were next to Carter. A photographer was snapping pictures.

All the responders looked up, acknowledging Rory and her with nods and muttered greetings as they got out of the cruiser and made their way to the murdered man. The body was still sitting up, propped against the sign, but his shirt had been pulled up to expose his torso. At first, Eden didn't see a message, only the blood and the stab wounds. But as she got closer, she spotted something.

The three numbers, 653.

"Mean anything to you?" the ME asked, looking up at them from his semistooped position over the body.

Eden repeated the numbers several times, but then shook her head. Rory did the same.

"I did a search of them on my phone," Judson explained. "I think it could be part of an address. Or rather it used to be the first three numbers of the address for the Devil's Hideout when it was still called a farm road."

Eden groaned. The site of the first two murders. But with the barn now reduced to rubble by the IED, maybe the killer wanted to use some of the address numbers to connect the trio of dead bodies.

"But it could also be the number of a case file," Judson went on. "I'm talking way back before any of our time on the force. Forty-three years ago," he said, reading notes from his phone. "Mellie and Frank Mott, who were both sixteen at the time, filed a report of someone firing a shot into the barn when they were inside it."

Eden was sure she gave him a blank look because this was the first she was hearing of such an incident. "A shooting at the Devil's Hideout barn?"

Judson nodded. "Of course, it wasn't called that back then, and apparently, Frank was working there as a part-time hand after school."

"So was Mellie, according to Frank," Eden remarked. "I'm guessing she was there for work?"

"It doesn't say, and the deputy who wrote the report, Cliff Marquez, died more than a decade ago," Judson explained. "But from the impression I get, I think Mellie and Frank must have been dating or just been friends, and she met him there after school. Someone fired a shot into the barn, but they never found out who, and in his notes Cliff didn't speculate as to who might have done it."

Eden looked at Rory to see if this was ringing any bells. Obviously, it wasn't. "I'll call Aileen later," he said, referring to his former boss, retired Sheriff Aileen Granger, who was Grace's mother.

Even though the incident had happened decades ago, Aileen was still as sharp as a tack and would almost certainly recall a shooting. She might even be able to speculate as to whether or not it was playing into the current murders.

They would also need to talk to Frank. And Eden was already dreading it. The man was uncooperative, and this wasn't going to improve things. However, Eden did find it interesting that they'd talked to Frank about when he'd worked with Mellie, and he hadn't mentioned a shooting. The odds were he simply hadn't forgotten something as serious as that.

Rory shifted his attention back to the ME and the body. "Can you give us an idea of time of death?"

"Within the past four hours," he answered. "No signs of a struggle. No defense wounds, but you saw the stun-gun marks?"

Eden and Rory nodded.

"There were four total," the ME added. "Those two on his neck and another set on his back." He eased the body forward a little, lifting the shirt to show them the two lesions.

So maybe the killer had sneaked up on him. But then why stun him twice? Unless the killer had wanted to immobilize Carter a second time after they'd arrived at the current location. That was the likely scenario since the first hit from the stun gun wouldn't have lasted that long.

"He was stabbed seven times, mainly in the chest and stomach," the ME continued after he'd maneuvered the body back against the sign post. "Not sure if one or more of the wounds hit anything vital, but I'll be able to determine that in the postmortem. My guess is the numbers were carved after he was dead." He looked up at his assistant, who'd been taking the photos. "Let's go ahead and get the body back to the morgue so I can get started on—"

The ME stopped, interrupted by a strange hissing sound.

"What the hell?" Judson muttered, and like Eden, Rory and Garrison, he was glancing all around them, looking for the source.

And they soon saw it.

About five yards away in the ditch, a fire ignited. It had been barely noticeable at first. But it didn't stay that way. It soon soared up into a high flame. A flame that didn't stay contained to that one spot. It burst out in all directions.

Mercy.

It was coming right at them like a giant fireball.

They all started running, but Eden glanced over her shoulder to make sure they weren't about to be gunned down. She couldn't see anything, including the bomb squad, because of the thick black smoke billowing out from the flames.

What the heck was this?

Maybe some kind of incendiary IED? If so, no one had stepped on it. And no one had been near it since they'd arrived on scene. So it could have been on some kind of timer.

And if there was one, there could be more.

Eden quickly got confirmation of that theory when two more fires ignited. One of the other side of the road and one in the ditch right next to the responder vehicles. Smoke was coming at them from multiple sides now, and she could even feel the heat from the flames licking through the air.

"I called the fire department," Judson shouted. "They're on the way. I told them to approach with caution."

Good. Eden hadn't seen any IEDs on the road itself, but that didn't mean there weren't any.

A fourth fire burst to life in the ditch practically right next to Rory and her. That gave her another jolt of adrenaline and sent her already accelerated heartbeat racing even more. She couldn't breathe. Couldn't see.

But she could hear.

And she heard something she definitely didn't want to hear.

Gunshots.

Rory took hold of her arm and pulled her down on the road, trying to keep her out of the line of fire. She prayed the others were doing the same thing.

On her belly now, Eden drew her gun and lifted her head just enough so she could continue to look around. Beside her, Rory was doing the same, and like her, he was obviously trying to pick through the smoke to see their attacker so they could return fire and stop this.

But nothing.

More shots came. All at once. Dozens of them.

And they seemed to be coming from multiple directions. Sweet heaven. How many shooters were there? Had the killer sent a small army after them? If so, she wasn't sure how they were going to escape. Every one of them could be killed right here.

The image of Tyler flashed through her mind, and she added more prayers. That her precious little boy was safe, that this wasn't some two-pronged attack, where gunmen were at the ranch to go after him.

Eden dug out her phone from her pocket, and since she wasn't even sure she'd be able to hear Grace, she sent her a text. Under attack here at the latest murder scene. Is everything okay there?

Everything's fine here, Grace quickly texted back. Update me about the attack as soon as you can.

Eden would do just that. If they made it out of this alive.

"Do you see the shooters?" Garrison called out. It was hard to hear him with the barrage of shots slamming through the air and all around them.

Garrison was somewhere to her left, which meant he was closer to the ditch. Maybe another of those fire devices wouldn't be going off there.

A bullet smacked into the road just a couple of inches from her, sending up some small pieces of asphalt. The projectiles flew through the air, one of them slicing across the sleeve of her shirt.

It'd come close.

Too close.

But she couldn't say the same for most of the other shots. They seemed to be landing everywhere. So either the shooters had lousy aim, or...

Eden didn't get to finish that train of thought because Rory finished it for her.

"I don't think it's gunmen," Rory said, shouting to be heard about the deafening racket. "I think bullets have been planted in the fires."

Yes, Eden realized that was exactly what was happening. The term was "cooking off" when ammunition was heated up enough in a fire to cause them to discharge. It didn't make the situation less deadly, but it could mean there wasn't actually a shooter nearby.

Could.

It was possible there was indeed a sniper, waiting to finish the job if the heated bullets didn't kill them.

"Everyone stay down," Rory shouted, and Eden saw him glancing in the direction of the cruiser.

He was no doubt wondering if they could make it there. Maybe. But if they stood, it would make them an easier target for those random shots.

In the distance, she heard the sound of a fire engine and hoped none of the responders would get hurt when they approached. Rory must have been concerned about the same thing because he took out his phone and called Dispatch to have their situation relayed to the fire chief.

Another fire shot up on the side of the road just ahead,

and it didn't take long before bullets started going off there, too. It seemed to go on for an eternity, but she knew it was probably less than two minutes before the fire engine roared to a stop not far from the other vehicles.

The crew didn't immediately get out, and when they did, they were wearing helmets and vests that she was pretty sure were bullet-resistant. More minutes crawled by, the hail of bullets continuing, while the firefighters hooked up the hose. The moment they'd done that, they started dousing the flames.

Since the fires weren't huge, they weren't that difficult to put out, but there were four of them, so it took a while. Second by second, though, the sound of the gunfire began to trail off.

Rory and she stayed put, waiting. Hoping. Praying.

"Is anyone hurt?" Rory shouted.

"Okay, here," the ME said. And one by one, the others reported in. All except Garrison.

"I took a bullet to the leg," the deputy finally said, prompting Rory and her to start scrambling in his direction. Depending on the location of the injury, he could bleed out.

"Ambulance is on the way," Judson told them, and he hurried over.

One look at the young deputy, and Eden knew it was bad.

Chapter Fourteen

Rory paced across the guestroom while he listened to the latest update on Garrison. The deputy was alive, barely, but, according to Bennie, Garrison had been medevacked to a medical center in San Antonio, where he was in critical condition.

At least he was alive. And Rory was clinging to the hope he'd recover.

What he didn't have a lot of hope about at the moment was that they'd be able to stop the killer from launching another attack. But he was working on it. Eden, too, but they'd opted to do that at Dutton's rather than return to the police station. This way, they could be near Tyler.

Right now, they needed that.

After they'd dealt with the mop-up of yet another crime scene, they'd come back to the ranch and set up a makeshift office in one of the guestrooms. Tyler was just across the hall in the nursery with Leslie, and Eden and he had been popping over there all afternoon. They'd continue to do that even though Tyler was down for the night in his crib. But for now, they had the monitor on, and it was on the end table of a sitting area where they both could see it.

He finished his call with Bennie, knowing if there was a change in Garrison's condition, that Bennie or someone else would let them know. Rory put away his phone and looked at Eden. She was sitting on the floor, her back against the small sofa, and she was volleying glances between him, her laptop screen and the baby monitor.

"Garrison's in ICU," he disclosed. Rory had already shut the guestroom door so their calls and conversations wouldn't disturb anyone, meaning there was no reason for him to whisper. "And he's still critical."

She sighed and closed her eyes a moment. "He's barely twenty-two years old," she muttered.

Yeah, by far the youngest currently on the police force. That ate away at Rory. But then, a lot of things were eating away at him right now.

He tipped his head to her phone, which was on the floor next to her. "Any luck getting in touch with Aileen?" They needed to ask her about that shooting incident at the barn. They'd opted out of bringing it up to Frank until they had Aileen's take on it.

Eden shook her head. "I left her a voice mail. Grace said her mom was in San Antonio visiting friends, and she often turns off her phone while she's there."

That eased some of his tension. When Aileen hadn't answered their initial call, he'd been concerned that something might have happened to her, but if this was her norm, then maybe she was all right. He wouldn't breathe easier about that, though, until he heard from her.

"A report came in a couple of minutes ago from the bomb squad," Eden informed him.

Rory went to her, and since she was on the floor, that's where he sat, too, and he soon saw that the report was three pages, and she was on the last one. Eden had obviously been reading it while he was getting the update on Garrison.

She moved the laptop closer to him and started the recap. "Each of the fires were ignited with small incendiary devices triggered by a remote. Maybe even a cell phone. The devices had been placed in holes in the ground from when there used to be underground mineral springs in that area."

Rory knew about those holes. Knew, too, that some of them could be quite wide and deep. On the surface, most of them looked like gopher holes or just shallow depressions in the ground, but sometimes when people stepped in them, they'd end up with a broken foot or leg. Obviously, the killer had known about the holes, too.

And had made use of them.

"The IEDs were positioned over a mix of plastic bottles filled with gasoline and boxes of bullets," Eden went on. "Dried leaves and grass had likely been used to cover the holes so they wouldn't be easily visible."

Rory considered that. The items themselves wouldn't be that hard to get, but it would have taken time to plant all of that. And the rigging wouldn't have necessarily happened this morning. No. The killer could have set all of that up earlier before he or she had brought Carter there.

"It was all a huge risk," Rory muttered.

"Yes," she agreed. "But it wouldn't have taken much strength," Eden added. "Which means it doesn't rule out Diedre or Helen."

No, it did not, and Rory could see how this might have played out. "All three of the victims could have been lured to the places where they were killed. No lifting or dragging required for the killer. Just get them there and murder them. In Mellie's and Brenda's cases, the killer could have even been reasonably sure they wouldn't be interrupted by someone just passing by."

"Not the case with Carter, though," Eden murmured.

"True, but since it was dark, the killer might have parked off the road and dropped down into the ditch if they saw headlights. That was still a risk, but if someone had stopped, then that person might have been killed, too."

It twisted at his gut to think of that possibility, but this killer hadn't had an issue with collateral damage. One CSI was already dead, and a deputy was clinging to life. So, yes, killing any potential witnesses could have happened.

Eden stayed quiet a moment. "Any of our suspects could have done this," she said on a groan.

Again, she was right. Because none of them, including Ike, had an actual alibi for the time of Carter's death.

When Eden groaned again, he turned to her, and Rory automatically pulled her into his arms. Just touching her helped with this tangle of nerves and spent adrenaline, and she dropped her head on his shoulder.

Her breath was slow and rhythmic, hitting against his neck. Almost like a kiss. His body thought so, anyway, but his body didn't get a chance to fuel that fantasy, or actually kiss her, because Eden's phone buzzed with a call.

"It's Aileen," she said, glancing at the screen, answering the call. "You're on speaker and Rory is here with me," she told Aileen.

"I figured he would be. I just spoke with Grace, and she filled me on what's been going on. I hope I'm not calling too late."

"No," Eden assured her, though it was past nine, not a common time for a phone call in a town where people often went to bed early and got up early, but then there wasn't anything common about this situation. "Did Grace tell you we wanted to ask you about the shooting incident at the barn back when Mellie and Frank were teenagers?"

"She did," Aileen confirmed. "And even though it wasn't my case, I remember that Mellie was the one who reported it. She called it into the station, and she was upset and crying. Cliff Marquez responded and came back a couple of hours later, and he went over the details. Mellie and Frank were basically making out in one of the stalls, and someone fired a shot into the barn."

"Did they see who?" Rory asked.

"No, but Mellie thought it was Helen," Aileen said.

Everything inside Rory went still. "That wasn't in the report."

"It wasn't." Aileen huffed. "Because as you're aware, Helen's family had money and influence. Her father claimed she wasn't anywhere near the barn, and since there was no evidence to prove otherwise, Cliff had to let her go. And while I don't know this for sure, I believe Cliff caved to pressure from Helen's folks to keep her name out of it."

"But you believe Helen might have done it," Eden concluded.

"Believed it but couldn't prove it," Aileen said quickly. "Mellie said she'd seen Helen about a half hour earlier, and she was glaring at Frank and her as they were making their way to the barn. I suspect there was some kind of jealousy or love triangle going on, and Helen was a hothead back then. Still is," she added.

Rory had to agree with that. Both Ike and Helen were cut from the same cloth when it came to temperament. And holding grudges.

"Did Frank believe Helen had fired the shot?" Rory queried.

"If he did, he didn't voice it to Cliff or anyone else that I know of. Back then, though, Frank wasn't what I would call a wave maker. He was a star wrestler. A jock. Very popular in high school, and he loved the girls. Not for long, though, since he seemed to leave a trail of broken hearts. Until he met his wife, that is."

"Was Helen one of his broken-heart relationships?" Eden asked.

"I think so," Aileen said after a short hesitation. "Helen moved away when Frank got married, and she rarely came back to town. Then, after Miranda died, Helen started showing up again. I'm not sure she was actually in love with Frank. More like he was that guy Helen just couldn't get out of her system."

Rory made the mistake of glancing at Eden just as she was glancing at him. And he saw it in her eyes. They hadn't been able to get each other out of their systems, either, so he knew how Helen felt.

Man, he knew.

The heat was always there. Always. If it'd been just the attraction, he might have been able to put that on the back burner. But there were these deep feelings he'd had for her since, well, for as long as he'd known her. Some might say she was his soul mate, but Rory knew that Eden would always be the love of his life.

"Both Helen and Frank have had relationships over the years," Aileen went on, snapping Rory's attention back to her, "but they always seemed to find their way back to each other." She stopped again. "And that has to have you wondering if Helen's obsession with Frank is playing into the murders."

It was indeed. "Mellie had been involved with Frank, and she's dead," Rory explained. "But I can't find any indications that Frank and Mellie had resumed their teenage romance."

"It doesn't have to have been a real relationship for

Helen to believe it was," Aileen pointed out. "Frank was spending a lot of time going to Mellie to complain about the foster kids. Helen might have seen that as Frank's attempts to spend time with Mellie and maybe win her back."

Yes, that was possible. Then, Helen might have killed Mellie in a jealous rage. But how did the other two murders play into this? The only thing Rory could think of was that Helen had maybe decided to keep going and try to pin the murders on Ike. Then again, all three murders could have been designed for that right from the start, and jealousy might not have anything to do with this.

"I know this shooting happened a long time ago," Rory said to Aileen, "but I want to use it and the other circumstantial evidence that we have to get a search warrant for Helen's house."

Aileen made a sound of agreement. "I can help with that if you want."

"I do. Thanks." Rory wasn't going to turn down an offer like that. Aileen still had a lot of support in town, and even though the former sheriff would never bend the law, she would be able to cut through the red tape much faster than he could.

"All right. I'll get right on that," Aileen assured him. "Are you going to talk to Frank and ask him about the shooting?"

"I am. Thanks again, Aileen." Rory ended the call and immediately pressed Frank's number. It took four rings before the man finally answered.

"It's late, Deputy McClennan," Frank snapped. He'd obviously seen Rory's name on the screen.

Rory didn't bother with an apology, and he got right to the point. "Think back to that shooting in the barn when you were a teenager. Do you believe Helen could have been the one to fire that shot?"

Frank was silent for so long that Rory wasn't sure the man was going to answer, but he finally said, "Yes."

"Any reason you didn't tell the cops that?" Rory asked.

"It would have only made matters worse. And the shot wouldn't have hit Mellie or me since it was fired into the hayloft. We weren't in any kind of real danger."

"Maybe, but someone shot at you," Rory reminded him. "I'd think you would want to say who did that."

"I didn't have any proof," Frank insisted. "It would have been my word against Helen's. Her family had power and money. Mine didn't. I would have likely ended up losing my job, and my name would have been mud in Renegade Canyon."

Rory wished that wasn't true. But it was.

"If you truly thought Helen had fired the shot, why did you continue to see her over the years?" Rory asked.

Frank sighed. "Helen was there for me after my wife died. I was an emotional mess, and if I hadn't had Helen, I wouldn't have gotten through it. I owe her. She also helped me get my ranch. She used her family's influence to get me the best deal possible on the place and even lent me part of the down payment."

Rory thought of what Aileen had said about Helen not being able to let go of Frank, but it seemed to Rory that the same could be said of Frank. He didn't press the man on his feelings for Helen. Instead, he went in a different direction.

"Will you voluntarily agree to a search of your house?" Rory asked. "I could get a warrant," he added.

Frank muttered some profanity. "Do the search. I consent to it," he said, surprising Rory. "Just not tonight because I'm about to head to bed. But you can send someone out first thing in the morning."

"Thank you," Rory said, but he was talking to the air because Frank had already ended the call.

"That was easier than expected," Eden muttered. She stayed quiet a moment. "You're mentally comparing Helen and Frank to you and me."

He nodded. Then shook his head. "I don't think you'd shoot at me if I was with another woman."

She surprised him by smiling. "Well, I might have when we'd been teenagers. Especially if you'd been with Tracy Muldoon."

He smiled, too, because Tracy had been the head cheerleader, and she'd made no secret that she wanted to replace Eden as his girlfriend. Tracy had done that via the mean-girl route of making Eden's life miserable in high school.

Her expression turned serious, and the levity of the moment was gone. "No, even then I wouldn't have shot at you."

She hadn't needed to spell that out. "We were both cops in the making even back then."

"Yes," she muttered, and she didn't take her gaze off him.

The energy and the heat between them went up a notch, and that's why Rory didn't kiss her. Didn't touch her. If he did, there'd be no turning back.

But then, Eden leaned in and kissed him.

Not a sweet peck on the mouth, either. She really kissed him, instantly making it long and deep. Instantly cranking up that heat and energy even more.

Rory was about to issue a warning that his resolve wasn't that strong right now, but Eden didn't give him a chance. Hard to talk when they were French kissing. And when things were escalating to beyond just this kiss.

Turning, Eden moved her leg over him and shifted her position until she was on his lap. That didn't just amp up the heat. It caused it to skyrocket, and it snapped every bit of his restraint. It suddenly didn't matter that sex could turn out to be a mistake.

Nope.

Because it was going to happen.

That was the problem, and the huge advantage, of being with someone whose body and mind he knew so well. Rory could feel this wasn't just a kiss to soothe. This wasn't about soothing at all. It was about feeling. It was about needing.

It was about them.

He slid his arm around her, snapping Eden closer to him, until her breasts were pressed against his chest. And he did some escalating of his own. The kiss went from hot to scalding. The need went from urgent to an absolute necessity.

Rory had to have her now.

Thankfully, Eden seemed to feel the same way.

She took those scalding kisses to his neck, doling out some torture and pleasure with the flick of her tongue over his skin. She knew all his hot spots. Hell, she'd been the one to discover them since they'd been each other's firsts. They had a long history of torture and pleasure.

Needing to do some kissing of his own, Rory turned the tables on her and went after her breasts. Eden's hot spots. He pushed up her top, shoved down the bra and used his mouth and tongue on her nipples.

Eden moaned, that sound of pleasure he knew all too well. A sound that shot through every part of his body. Especially one part that was urging him to move faster. To take everything she was offering.

Rory did just that, and he pulled off her top. Rid her of the bra, too. And the battle began. Because the clothes were obviously the enemy now, and they wanted each other naked.

Even then, the kissing and touching didn't stop, and somehow they managed not to injure themselves when the battle of the clothing escalated. Eden yanked off his shirt, sliding some tongue kisses on his chest while she fumbled with his jeans.

Rory ended up helping her with that, which led to some rolling around on the floor while holsters, boots and jeans all came off. The frantic pace continued when they were naked—their mouths met again, and the kiss roared past the hungry stage. The pleasure and need consumed him, and he was ready to take her here and now, but Eden said something that got through his lust-hazed mind.

"Condom," she muttered through her gusting breath.

Hell. He'd nearly forgotten again, and the last time, he'd gotten her pregnant. Since he doubted she wanted that to happen again, he forced himself to move away from her and locate his jeans. Then, his wallet. Then, the condom he kept there.

Eden made her way toward him, and the second he had the condom on, she straddled him, taking her inside him. The pleasure wasn't just a roar now. It was an avalanche of all the sensations that confirmed to him that this wasn't a mistake.

Eden was the right woman.

And despite the investigation, it was the right time.

Eden started the maddening strokes, taking him deep inside her, and he could see the pleasure on her face. Could feel it in her body as he slid his hands down her breasts and stomach. She rode him, drawing out every bit of that pleasure. Building it. Making them both climb.

And desperate.

Because that's what happened with great sex. The need became overwhelming, impossible to stave off. But Rory held on, savoring it. Savoring her. And when Eden's body finally found the release, Rory let himself take the plunge with her.

Yeah, this was right.

Chapter Fifteen

Eden stood in the shower and let the pulsing jets go to work on her tight muscles. She was sore and bruised and had some scrapes from both the barn explosion and having to dive onto the road after the firebombs.

The romp on the floor with Rory had maybe added a few new bruises, but the sex had made that all worth it. In fact, the sex had made a lot of things worth it.

Including the doubts and regrets.

Being with Rory had definitely muddied the waters of their already complicated relationship, but there was no chance of regretting it. She'd needed him, and he'd given her exactly what Rory was capable of giving.

Which was pretty much everything.

Rory cared for her. He loved their son. And he was a good man. Soon, she was going to have to decide if being with him was worth the daily battles that Ike would dole out. Then again, if Ike was in jail, then he couldn't make trouble for them.

But she still couldn't see Ike committing these murders.

No, and that meant eventually the evidence would clear his name. Eventually, the real killer would be caught and put in jail. And then life would get back to…

"Normal," she muttered.

That should have made her feel better, but there were some question marks on catching the killer. It was possible that once the killer had run through the list of Ike's enemies, the murders would stop. There might never be justice for Mellie, Brenda or Carter.

And as for going back to normal?

That might not happen. Not after these emotional barriers had come down between Rory and her. They might never go back to the way things had been just a few days ago. Now, she needed to decide how she felt about that.

With that thought weaving its way through her mind, she stepped out of the shower to a variety of sounds. She could hear Rory and Tyler on the baby monitor that she'd brought into the bathroom with her after they'd all had breakfast with Dutton, Grace, Leslie and Nash. Tyler and Rory were now back in the nursery, and her son was babbling while Rory was reading to him.

But there was another sound—her buzzing phone.

And on the monitor she could hear Rory's buzzing as well.

Despite her son's happy sounds, the dread raced through her, and she steeled herself to hear more bad news. She prayed there hadn't been another murder.

It wasn't that early, already a little past ten, and Livvy and Bennie had been sending them text updates, but this was the first call of the morning.

She looked at her phone screen and saw not only Livvy's name, but also that it was a group call to Bennie, Rory and her. On the monitor, she heard Rory answer, muttering to Livvy that he was going to leave Tyler with Leslie in the nursery and step out in the hall so they could talk.

Eden answered as well, putting it on speaker so she could dry off and get dressed in the clothes that Dutton had

had brought over from her place. She needed to be ready since it was possible she and Rory would be leaving soon to put out another fire.

Maybe a literal one.

"I'm here," Eden said to the group. "Did something happen?"

"No one else is dead," Livvy answered, clearly picking up on Eden's concern. "But I thought you should know about the latest on Garrison. And the searches that are going on as we speak at Frank's and Helen's."

Yes, she definitely wanted to hear about Garrison. Eden had known about Aileen coming through on the search warrant. They'd gotten that info in a text while they were eating breakfast. Aileen had also let them know that SAPD would be the ones executing the warrant and sending in their own CSIs, so none of the deputies would have to go into San Antonio to do it. But Eden hadn't been aware that the actual searches would take place so soon.

"Garrison's still in ICU," Livvy began, "but his condition is improving. The doctors are a lot more optimistic about his condition now than they were last night. They believe he's going to make it."

Good. Eden hoped that he made a full recovery, and once he was out of ICU, she would try to go see him.

"I haven't heard anything back yet on Helen's search," Livvy went on, "but Bennie wants to give us an update about what he found at Frank's."

"Or rather what I didn't find," Bennie interjected. She heard the man huff. "I know in one of the reports that Helen said Frank had lots of magazines about guns and explosives, but we didn't find anything like that anywhere in his house. In fact, no magazines, just a handful of nonfiction books about histories of various wars."

"Maybe Frank hid or destroyed them?" Eden suggested.

"Yeah, I considered that so I checked the attic and any possible hidey-hole I could think of. Nothing there, and there were no fresh ashes in the fireplace or the barbecue grill," Bennie informed them. "The man's not a pack rat, that's for sure. There was practically nothing in the attic. That minimalism applied to the house, too. No clutter, everything in its place and I didn't see a spot where a bunch of magazines had once been. Of course, that doesn't mean he didn't get rid of them before I showed up."

"True," Rory agreed, "but it also could mean Helen was lying. And there's only one reason I can think of for her doing that. She wants Frank to look guilty."

"I think I'm going with that option," Bennie muttered. "While I was looking around, Frank and I chatted, and I got the feeling the man was scared of Helen. Maybe not actually scared for himself but for anyone who crossed her."

"Diedre," Rory and Eden said in unison. It was Eden who continued. "Both Frank and Diedre want to keep their relationship a secret, but if Helen found out, she might have wanted to get back at Frank by making him look guilty." She stopped, groaned. "Has anyone checked in with Diedre this morning?"

There were more groans. "I'll do that now," Livvy said. "Just stay on the phone with Bennie, and I'll use a landline."

"Bennie, did Frank happen to mention Diedre?" Eden asked after Livvy had left the group chat.

"He didn't bring her up, but she's something else I worked into the conversation while I was searching. I asked him the last time he saw her, and get this—he said it was night before last."

"The night of Brenda's murder," Eden muttered. It was

also when Carter had taken those photos of Diedre returning home in different clothes.

"Yep. That puts Diedre in Renegade Canyon at the time of the attack," Bennie said. "Well, it does if Frank is telling the truth."

And that was the problem with this investigation. Someone was lying, since Diedre had said she wasn't in town that night. Unfortunately, Eden didn't think they were going to get the truth from the killer.

But what exactly was the truth?

"Diedre's not answering her phone," Livvy said, coming back on the line. "Should I have SAPD check on her?"

"Yes," Rory said immediately, and Eden knew why.

If Diedre wasn't the killer, then she could be the next target. Then again, the same could be said about Rory and her.

"Did anything else turn up in the search of Frank's house?" Rory asked, obviously directing that question at Bennie.

"Not a thing." But then the deputy paused. "It seemed too clean. Maybe that's just Frank's thing, and I could way off base here, but to me it looked as if everything might have been…staged," he said. She heard him gather his breath. "I'm about to check in with SAPD on the search at Helen's. If anything turns up, I'll let you know."

Rory thanked Livvy and him, and he ended the call. Seconds later, just as Eden was putting on the rest of her clothes, there was a knock at the bathroom door.

"It's me," Rory said.

She opened it, and despite the serious conversation they'd just had, Eden had to deal with the stomach flutters she got whenever she was around Rory. The flutters must have shown on her face because the corners of Rory's mouth lifted.

"You do the same to me," he muttered, and then he leaned in and melted her with a kiss.

She was toast.

No way could she not sink into that kiss and make it last a whole lot longer and turn a whole lot hotter than it should be. Apparently, she was going to continue to muddy these relationship waters with him.

He eased back, that slight smile still in place on his clever mouth, and he smoothed his hand over her cheek. Again, she must not have had a poker face because he seemed to know exactly what she was thinking.

"Let's not overthink this," he muttered.

"Good. Because I don't believe I can cram anything else into my head right now." Eden didn't get a chance to add more because their phones buzzed again, and this time it was Bennie who'd initiated the call.

"The CSIs going through Helen's house found something," Bennie blurted the moment they answered. "And it's not good."

Eden and Rory both groaned, and Eden could think of many incriminating things they could find in the house of a possible killer. "What?" Rory asked.

"They found some traces of the supplies that were used to make those IEDs," Bennie explained. "They were in a plastic bag at the bottom of her trash can."

Rory's gaze met hers, and she saw the relief. And the sickening dread. They might finally have their killer, but it was horrific to think of his blood kin committing these horrible crimes.

"There are also some deleted computer searches on how

to make explosives," Bennie added. "Her laptop will be sent to the lab to see what else they can find on it."

"They're certain it's the same supplies as those in the IEDs?" Rory asked.

"They seem plenty certain to me. Of course, everything will be tested, but they had the components of the IEDs from the bomb-squad guys and matched them to what they found in that plastic bag."

Rory stayed quiet a moment, obviously processing that revelation. "What did Helen have to say about that bag and the computer searches?"

Bennie huffed. "She's not here. According to the CSIs, she left shortly after the search began. And they say she's not answering her phone."

"Hell," Rory grumbled. "Put out an APB on Helen. I wanted her found *now*."

Rory tried not to curse when he read the latest text from Detective Vernon. Tried and failed. Because it wasn't good news.

Still no sign of Helen.

It'd been hours since his aunt had walked out of her house during a CSI search. Hours since the CSIs had found the components that had been used to make those deadly IEDs. And after she'd walked out, Helen had seemingly vanished.

Was she out setting up another murder?

Or had Helen been set up by someone who'd planted that plastic bag in her trash bin? Her outdoor trash bin that was on the side of her garage where anyone could have gotten to it.

Either of those were possible, but Rory couldn't ask her about them because she couldn't be found.

He looked over at Eden and showed her the text from the detective. She seemed to be on the verge of cursing, too.

"I'm not having any better luck," she told him.

She was seated at Grace's desk at the police station, with not one but two laptops in front of her. One was for the reports and updates that seemed to be coming in nonstop—Rory was dealing with those and fielding the calls. Eden was using the other laptop to review the traffic camera feed around Helen's neighborhood to see if she could spot anyone coming or going from Helen's house.

"The problem is there isn't a traffic cam right at her subdivision," Eden explained. "The closest one is a quarter of a mile away so even if I don't see, say, Diedre or Frank, it doesn't mean they weren't there. They could have just used an alternate route."

Yeah, and if one of them was the killer, they might have scoped out where the cameras were and made sure to avoid them.

Rory heard the dinging sound on the second laptop, an indication that a new report had arrived, so he dropped down in the chair he'd pulled next to Eden's and saw the latest from Livvy.

Again, he had to clamp down the urge to curse.

"No unusual withdrawals from Helen's bank account," he advised Eden. "Ditto for Ike, Diedre and Frank."

Eden stopped the traffic camera feed and looked at him. "These weren't expensive attacks. Well, unless one of them hired someone to make the IEDs. But any of them could have made smaller withdrawals for that months in advance so it wouldn't send up any red flags."

"True. And Helen, Ike, Frank and Diedre all should have

known they'd be persons of interest or suspects for these killings."

"Ike," Eden repeated under her breath. "Where is he? He's not missing, too, is he?"

"He's not. He's at his lawyers' firm. He'll be coming back in soon to finish up his interview with Livvy." Though Rory wasn't holding out much hope they'd get anything useful from him.

Rory checked the time and saw they'd been at this for going on six hours now. It was midafternoon, and Eden looked more than ready for a break. He was about to suggest calling in an order from the diner up the street, but his phone rang.

"Diedre," he told Eden, and he took the call on speaker. "Where are you?" Rory demanded.

The woman huffed loud enough for him to hear it. Rory could also hear a car engine, which meant she was likely driving. "Look, I'm tired of you calling and leaving me messages. Can't you just leave me in peace?"

"No," he snarled, "and I wouldn't have to keep calling you if you'd just answer your phone. FYI, you're on speaker, and Deputy Gallagher is with me."

"Of course, she is," Diedre groaned. "She left me a voice mail, too."

Eden had indeed done that, but that had been hours ago. "Where are you?" Rory repeated.

Another loud huff. "I'm driving back from a business meeting. And, no, you don't need to verify if I had one or not because I mixed up the dates. The meeting isn't until next week. When I realized that, I turned around, and now, I'm heading back home. Why are you calling me?" she snorted.

Rory had a couple of things he needed to ask her, but he went with the most important one. "Where is Helen?"

"How should I know...?" But she stopped at what had sounded as if it might be a rant. "Is something wrong?"

"That's what I'm trying to find out. She's not answering her phone. Has she been in touch with you?"

"No." And now, Diedre sounded concerned. Of course, that might be a pretense. "I can try to call her."

"Do that once you answer a few more questions." And Rory went with the second thing on his list. "Were you at Frank's two nights ago?"

"No," she blurted, but again, she stopped. "Sorry, that's a knee-jerk reaction. It's become second nature to deny I've been with Frank. But, yes, I was there. Briefly," she added. "I was out for a drive and dropped by to see if he was busy. He was. He said he had a Zoom meeting with a cattle broker."

"So you were in Renegade Canyon when Brenda was attacked?" Rory made sure he used his cop's tone on that one.

"Good grief, you just don't give up, do you?" She didn't wait for him to respond to that. "Yes, I was there. Again, it was very brief. I went to Frank's, talked to him for a couple of minutes and then I left. That's it. I didn't stop off on the way home to murder a woman I hardly knew."

"But you did know her," Rory argued. "You had lunch with her. The two of you discussed your mutual hatred for Ike."

"So what?" Diedre growled at him. "I discussed that with Helen, too. And Frank. I haven't murdered either of them."

The sarcasm dripped from her voice, but Rory felt the icy chill go through him, and he resisted muttering "not yet."

"Are you done accusing me of things I didn't do?" Diedre snapped.

"No," he snapped right back, and Rory moved on to the final thing on his list. "Think back to a couple of months ago to a fight that took place between Frank and Ike at the cemetery."

"That," she choked out, and the sarcasm was gone. In its place was a hefty amount of anger. "That's when Ike acted like his usual SOB self and upset Frank."

"Were you there?" Rory asked.

"No, but Frank told me all about it," Diedre insisted, and he didn't have to prompt the woman to continue. She just started spewing out the venom. "Ike's a vile monster. First, he cheated on his wife with a lot of women. Yes, that included me, but I wasn't married at the time. But he also cheated with Frank's wife. And then he rubbed the cheating in Frank's face."

"You know this for sure?" Rory asked.

"I know Ike, and he doesn't care who he hurts. And he hurt Frank that day at the cemetery." The woman's voice cracked on those last words.

Rory jumped right on that. "How did he hurt him?"

Diedre didn't say anything for a long time. "Ike was there visiting your mom's grave, and Frank was clear on the other side of the cemetery visiting Miranda's. Ike made a point of walking over to him and blowing a kiss at Miranda's tombstone. Ike did that," she snorted. Not a shout. But the anger was there. So much anger.

If Ike had truly done that, and Rory didn't doubt that he had, then it was an SOB thing to do. Then again, Ike made a habit of doing whatever he could to hurt people. Nearly everyone in town had been on the receiving end of Ike's wrath at one time or another.

"What's wrong with him?" Diedre asked. "Is it just

plain meanness?" Again, she didn't wait for an answer, and she ended the call.

Rory and Eden sat in silence for a while, going over everything Diedre had just said. "That could be motive for the murders," Eden muttered.

Yeah, it could be, but it was motive for both Diedre and Frank. As for Helen, she had a motive of a different kind. To get rid of any competition she might have for Frank. That's why it was so critical for them to find her.

He took out his phone to try again to call her, but it rang before he could do that. "It's Ike's lawyer," he told Eden, and he figured Arnette was calling to reschedule his client's interview.

But Rory was wrong.

"Where's your father?" Arnette demanded the moment Rory answered. There was a frantic urge to the lawyer's normally cocky tone.

"He should be on his way here," Rory said. "Why?" And because he suddenly had a bad feeling about this, he put the call on speaker so Eden could hear as well.

"Because we had a meeting scheduled for well over an hour ago, and when Ike didn't show up or answer his phone, I started driving to the ranch. I figured he was maybe out riding or perhaps he'd lost track of time. But then I saw his truck," Arnette added, the strain in his voice going up a significant notch. "It was parked on a trail close to where that barn blew up."

An icy chill raced through Rory. Yeah, that bad feeling was warranted. "I take it he wasn't in the truck?" he asked, already standing. And Eden stood, too.

"No. He wasn't in it." Arnette's voice was shaking now. "But there was blood. So much blood." He made a loud groan. "Rory, I think somebody killed your father."

Chapter Sixteen

Eden was ready to take hold of Rory's arm to stop him from bolting out of the station and hurrying to get to Ike's truck.

But he thankfully didn't do that.

In fact, he muted the call with the lawyer and voiced the first thought that had occurred to her when she'd heard Arnette say "so much blood."

"This could be a trap," Rory muttered, and he fixed his gaze on her.

"Yes," she agreed. "One that the killer set, hoping we'd rush to the scene where we could be killed."

He nodded and unmuted his phone. "Arnette, move away from the truck and get back in your vehicle to wait for us. Walk backward, retracing your steps, because there could be IEDs."

That was highly likely since it had been the killer's preferred method in the previous attack. But Eden didn't doubt Ike had been taken.

Or hurt.

However, he was likely alive, for now, anyway, if the killer planned to use him as a lure. The killer could have taken Ike and then set up the explosives for anyone responding to the scene.

"An IED?" the lawyer repeated, and now there was

some serious panic in his voice to go along with the worry. Eden hoped that panic didn't send Arnette running because it could get him blown to bits.

"Get in your vehicle," Rory repeated. "But don't drive away."

Good advice, because if Arnette had pulled off the side of the road, he could hit an IED when he tried to leave.

"Stay put," Rory added. "Help will be there soon."

He ended the call, continuing to keep his gaze fixed on her, and then cursed. She knew the reason for his profanity, too, so Eden went ahead and spelled out what needed to happen.

"I'll go with you in a cruiser," she stated. "You can't leave me holed up here since the killer could just find another way to get to us. Let's try to end this now."

Oh, he didn't care for that, but Rory knew it was the right thing to do. Like him, it was her job to go after a killer.

He nodded, gave her one last look that was laced with worry and they went back into the squad room. Livvy, Judson and Bennie were all working at their desks, and they must have realized something was wrong because they got to their feet.

"Arnette found Ike's truck near the rubble of the old Sanderson barn," Rory explained. "There was blood. Eden and I will respond in one cruiser. Judson and Bennie, you'll go in a second one. Livvy, I need you here at the station. Call the bomb squad and get them out to the scene. Hell, the fire department, too, in case there are any more of those gasoline bombs. And let Grace and Dutton know what's going on."

"What about a roadblock?" Livvy asked.

"We'll do that after we arrive on scene, but get out the word that the road will be closed indefinitely."

Livvy nodded, already taking out her phone. "Where's Ike?"

"No idea," Rory said, and then motioned for Judson and Bennie to follow them, and they all headed outside.

Rory reached for the door handle of the cruiser and then stopped. "Check underneath for any explosives," he called out to Judson and Bennie.

That gave Eden a jolt because it was something that she hadn't even considered. But she sure as heck should have. With the cruisers just sitting there in the parking lot, the killer could have planted IEDs on the vehicles.

All four of them lowered to the ground, and they did a search of the undercarriage. Eden didn't see anything suspicious, but she didn't know if the killer had tucked it away, somewhere out of sight. Still, it would have been awfully bold to try to do something like that with the police station only a few yards away.

"Nothing," Judson said several moments later, and Rory echoed the same.

They got in their respective cruisers, and Eden suspected all of them were doing some praying when they started the engines. But thankfully, the cruisers didn't explode, so with sirens and lights on, they started toward the scene.

It was bold, too, for the killer to do anything in this area, since it had already been the scene of three murders. Then again, the CSIs were long gone, so maybe the killer figured that cops and responders wouldn't be around anytime soon. Still, it was gutsy.

"This isn't on the route from the ranch to town," Eden pointed out. "So what was Ike doing out here?"

"Maybe he was forced to come," Rory said without hesitation, letting her know he'd thought of the question, too. "The killer could have been waiting for him in his truck." He paused. "Or done something to lure him here. Hell, or even taken him from the house."

All of those possibilities could have happened. There was plenty of extra security at the ranch, but that was mainly around Dutton's house, and that was for protecting Tyler. Since the main house couldn't be seen from Dutton's, it was possible that someone had sneaked onto the grounds, waited and attacked Ike.

"Remember, too, that Ike came to Carter's scene because of that message he could save someone," Rory went on. "I doubt Ike would fall for that again, but it could have been a different tactic."

"Like what?" she asked.

He looked at her, and she saw the worry in his eyes. "The killer could have called for a showdown, a way for Ike to put an end to this. Ike might not have turned that down."

True. After all, Rory and she hadn't, and this could have all been put in place to get them killed. But something about that bothered her.

"If the killer's intentions are to flat-out murder us," she said, "then why not just shoot us when we were at the barn or when we were with Carter's body?"

Rory lifted his shoulder. "It could be that shooting isn't part of his or her skill set. We know Frank had firearms training in the military, but I don't have any idea how sharp his skills are. And I don't recall anything in Helen's or Diedre's background to indicate they're markswomen." He paused. "Then again, there's nothing to link Diedre to having the know-how to make explosives."

No, but there was that link to Helen. And perhaps one to

Frank, if Helen had been telling the truth about the magazines she saw. But even then, owning magazines like that didn't mean someone knew how to construct an IED.

Just in case the killer did decide to launch a sniper attack, Eden kept watch around them as they drove to the scene. It didn't take long, and they only passed one other vehicle during the five-minute drive.

She soon spotted Arnette's sleek silver Jaguar on the side of the road, and just as the man had said, Ike's truck was on one of the trails. Definitely not out of sight, though. In fact, it was barely on the trail itself, which meant the killer had likely wanted it to be found.

Rory pulled to a stop, not on the side of the road but right smack in the middle of it. He turned off the sirens but kept the lights on. Behind him, Judson did the same, and when Bennie and he got out, they all looked around on the road and the shoulder.

Nothing.

Well, nothing visible, anyway.

Eden took out two sets of latex gloves from the supply kit under her seat. She shoved one pair into her pocket, and Rory did the same to the pair she handed him.

"Get the roadblocks up," Rory told Judson and Bennie.

The two deputies went straight to the trunk and brought out the bright yellow plastic barricades. Livvy would send out a road crew to set up signs farther up, but this would do for now. At least there weren't any steep curves, so anyone traveling here would be able to see the barriers and the whirling blue cruiser lights in time to stop.

No repeats of what had happened to Rory and her with those strips of spikes.

Arnette didn't get out of his car as she and Rory approached, but he did lower his window a fraction. The lawyer was clearly rattled. He was sweating, and his hands were shaking.

"Is there a bomb?" Arnette blurted.

"Haven't had time to look yet, but I don't want you driving off. Go ahead and move to one of the cruisers. They're bullet-resistant."

That didn't ease the panicked look in Arnette's eyes, but with a shaky nod, he got out of the Jag and scurried toward a cruiser. There were no keys in the ignition, so the man wouldn't just be able to drive off. At least this way, though, he'd be semiprotected if all hell broke loose.

Again.

"Watch where you step," Rory muttered to her as they started toward Ike's truck. "And look for any footprints."

She did and so did Rory, along with firing lots of glances around them. As for spotting footprints, she soon realized that would be next to impossible. The entire surface here was fine gravel. It was perhaps why the killer had chosen it, since some of the other trails were dirt.

Rory went to the driver's side, and she went to the passenger's. Both doors were closed, but she had no trouble seeing what had alarmed Arnette.

The blood.

It was spattered on the windshield, the dash, the seat and the coffee mug that was in the cupholder. The total amount probably wasn't enough to indicate a fatal blood loss, but she could understand why Arnette had been so alarmed. The spatter likely meant Ike had received a blow to the head.

Or someone else had.

Because, after all, they had no idea if the blood was Ike's. He could have been involved in some kind of altercation and maybe had been the one who'd delivered such a blow. But if that was the case, where was he?

She slipped on one of the gloves and was about to open the door for a closer look, but Rory's warning of "no" came through loud and clear.

"The doors could be rigged with explosives," he reminded her.

Eden mentally cursed. Of course. That's something this killer could do to ensure their death.

After taking off the glove and shoving it back in her pocket, Eden settled for doing a visual of the interior and outside of the truck. There were way too many places where an explosive could have been set, and out of sight. Best to leave this for the bomb squad ,and eventually, the CSIs.

"More blood," Rory said. "It's on the ground."

She carefully went around the back of the truck so she could join him, and she followed his gaze to the drops on the gravel. Again, not a huge amount, but it looked as if the blood hadn't been there that long.

"And more," Rory added, pointing just ahead on the trail.

Eden saw, too, and went with him to the spot. It didn't take long before they saw more just ahead.

"This feels a little like following breadcrumbs," he muttered.

Yes, it did. Breadcrumbs that would lead them straight into an attack. That's why they both drew their guns and kept moving, slowly, checking for anything that could help them make sense of this scene.

If the killer had been leading Ike along this trail, then where was the killer's vehicle? It lent credence to the theory that the killer had been in Ike's truck and forced him here. Maybe that meant the killer had left some DNA or trace evidence inside the truck.

As they moved, she spotted one of those holes left over from the dried-up mineral springs. Unlike the ones the killer had used around Carter, this one was huge, a caved-in section of the ground the size of a bathtub. If the killer had planted IEDs in this one, she couldn't see them because it was too deep.

They kept moving, kept following the blood drops, but they both stopped when there was a sound.

A low, hoarse moan.

Maybe.

Since this was in the sticks by anyone's standards, it was possible an animal had made the sound. But Eden didn't believe that. No. The sound had been human. A human in pain.

Rory must have thought so, too, because he quickened the pace just a little, but he also continued to keep watch. Eden did the same.

And she heard it again.

That moan.

And thankfully, this time she could better pinpoint the location. It'd come from just ahead and to her right, where there was a cluster of thick cedars.

Because of the underbrush, they couldn't just step off the trail, where there might be explosives, so they continued ahead. When they reached the cedars, though, she didn't see Ike.

Not at first, anyway.

But then she spotted him.

And her heart dropped to her knees.

Because the blood was streaming down the side of Ike's head, and he appeared to be barely conscious. He was sitting, but he'd been tied to a tree. Not just his hands and feet. The rope had been coiled around his torso, anchoring him in place.

That wasn't all, though.

No.

Around him, mere inches away from where Ike sat, there was a perfect semicircle of something Eden hadn't wanted to see.

Four IEDs.

RORY SUCKED IN a hard breath and immediately glanced all around the area. Because even though the IEDs had gotten their attention, that didn't mean the killer wasn't going to try to capitalize on the distraction and kill them.

He took hold of Eden's arm, moving her next to one of the larger trees. As cover went, it sucked, but at least it was better than them standing out in the open.

"Ike?" Eden called out to his father while Rory texted Livvy to send an ambulance.

Of course, the EMTs wouldn't be able to get to Ike, not until the bomb squad had cleared the IEDs, but Rory wanted medical help on hand. Not just for Ike, but for anyone else who ended up hurt in this ordeal.

But what was the ordeal?

If the killer had used Ike to lure them to their deaths, then why put the IEDs in plain sight? Was it because the explosive devices were meant to be a distraction? If so, they were working. Hard to completely focus when the whole area might blow up.

"Ike?" Eden repeated.

This time, Ike struggled to get one of his eyes open. He was clearly dazed but alive. Not for long, though, if they didn't do something fast.

ETA on the bomb squad? he texted Livvy.

Fifteen minutes, she replied.

That time would no doubt crawl by, while Ike sat there, bleeding.

"Ike, who did this to you?" Eden asked.

His father turned to look at Eden, but Rory wasn't sure he was actually seeing her. There was blood in his left eye, and his face was a mask of pain with the one good eye barely open to a slit.

"Who did this?" she repeated.

Ike shook his head. "Someone hit me over the head when I got in my truck." Like his face, his voice was a tangle of pain as well. "I didn't see who." Blinking hard, he glanced around. "Where am I? How did I get here?"

Rory cursed. So Ike wasn't going to be able to tell them much, but the area around him offered a few clues. There were no drag marks, which meant the killer had carried Ike—which would eliminate Diedre because of her size. And while Helen was strong, he doubted even she could carry Ike.

That left Frank.

He could do the carrying, but that didn't mean he was the killer. Ike could have been bludgeoned and then drugged just enough to make him incapable of fighting back, but still able to walk. If so, the killer could have led him straight to this spot, tied him up and maybe given him another hit on the head or some drugs.

Which meant he couldn't rule out any of their suspects.

Heck, he couldn't even rule out Ike, who could have perhaps staged all of this. But that didn't feel right. There were easier ways for Ike to get to Eden and him.

Unless they weren't the targets.

Maybe he and Eden were the lures for someone else. For someone whom Ike wanted dead.

"Helen," Ike muttered.

And that sure as hell got Rory's attention. "What about her?" Rory demanded.

"Uh, she was here. Wasn't she?" Ike looked at him as if he might know the answer. Rory didn't.

"Where did you see her?" Eden asked.

Ike ran his tongue over his bottom lip and grimaced. "Here," he said but then shook his head. "Just up the trail."

Rory glanced in that direction, but he didn't see anyone. No surprise there. The narrow trail was jammed on both sides by trees and thick underbrush. Added to that, it curved around just about ten yards ahead. It was impossible to see who or what could be on the other side.

"Did Helen do this to you?" Eden asked.

Again, Ike shook his head. "Maybe. I don't know. I'm hurt. I need to get to the hospital."

"The ambulance will be here soon," Eden said. "How badly are you hurt? Is it just your head or do you have other injuries?"

Ike seemed to consider that a moment. "I'm not sure. Can't think straight, and everything's a blur."

So if he wasn't lying or faking, Ike either had a serious concussion or he'd indeed been drugged. It could be both, and he could even have brain damage. Again, that was true if this wasn't all some ploy.

But Rory was positive that the blood was the real deal.

And it was continuing to seep down the side of Ike's head.

Rory whirled around at the sound of footsteps, and the adrenaline shot through him. Unnecessarily, though, because it was Bennie.

"Judson's keeping an eye on the road and Arnette..." Bennie said, but his words trailed off when he got a glimpse of Ike and those IEDs. "Hell," he muttered.

That summed up Rory's feelings, too, and he debated their next step. If Helen was indeed somewhere on the trail, and she was the killer, Rory needed to neutralize her before the bomb squad arrived.

Especially if she had a detonator for those IEDs.

"Wait here for the bomb squad," Rory told Bennie, and he looked at Ike. "Don't move. Don't try to get out of those ropes. Don't even kick out your feet."

Because if he did, Ike would almost certainly set off one of the IEDs.

Ike muttered something that sounded like agreement. Whether it was or not, Rory needed to get moving.

"Eden, with me," he said, motioning for her to follow him up the trail. "I don't want to go too far," he added to her in a whisper. "I don't want to risk the killer going after Bennie."

"Yes," she answered so quickly that he understood that possibility had already occurred to her.

They didn't say anything else. They just took slow, cautious steps up the trail toward that blind curve while they tried to keep watch around them. He didn't know what game the killer was playing, but he sure as hell didn't like any part of this.

He paused for a moment when he heard something. A rustling sound in the bushes to his left. But moments later, a rabbit darted out and disappeared into the woods. Normally, that wouldn't have put a hard knot in his gut, but even a creature as small as a rabbit could set off one of those IEDs.

And there might be more than just the ones surrounding Ike.

Unlike the spot where Ike's truck had been left, this part of the trail wasn't nearly as visible from the road. The killer could have taken his time here. But when had she or he brought in the IEDs? Maybe that had been done during the night, and then they could have been positioned once Ike was here.

Rory drew in a long breath when he reached the curve, and even though he knew Eden wouldn't like it, he stepped in front of her, trying to shield her in case they were about to face down a killer.

Eden didn't balk, though. Instead, she turned to the side, watching their backs while they kept moving. Good. He didn't want them ambushed, and like that rabbit, the killer could be hiding in the underbrush, ready to spring.

But no one did.

And no one was on the other side of the curve, either.

Of course, that didn't mean Helen hadn't been here, but she could be long gone by now. Rory didn't think so, though. He was pretty sure they were being watched, but he couldn't see or hear anyone.

Not at first, anyway.

There was more of that rustling sound. Not on the trail, but to the left side of it. Bringing up his gun, he whipped in that direction, and spotted Helen.

She was there, standing by a tree.

And she had a gun.

Chapter Seventeen

Eden jolted when she saw Helen with that gun pointed at them, and she was already dropping to the ground, catching hold of Rory to pull him down with her. She wanted both of them out of the line of fire.

Mercy, her heart had jumped to her throat, and it wasn't budging. It was stuck there like a rock. Of course, she'd known the killer could be Helen, but it still had been a shock to see her and that weapon.

Rory immediately rolled to the side and came up, taking aim at his aunt. "Put down your gun," he shouted.

But Helen didn't respond. Didn't move.

The woman stayed seemingly frozen there against the tree. No. Not frozen, Eden realized. But Helen was unable to move.

"I think she's been taped to the tree," Eden muttered.

The clear, wide kind of tape used for securing packages. It was hard to tell from this distance, but Eden thought she could see the light on the shiny surface. If that was it, then her neck had perhaps been taped as well, since her head was upright. The gun could be taped in place, too, since it was aimed outward, but Helen wasn't adjusting it so that it would be aimed at them.

"The killer could have put her here," Rory added.

Yes, that could have happened, but like Ike, this could be a ruse. A deadly one.

"Helen?" Rory shouted.

There was still no response, and the woman still wasn't trying to shift that gun around and shoot them. Was she waiting for them to get closer so she could get a better shot? Heck, was she even alive? Unlike Ike, there was no blood, but there were no obvious signs of life, either.

"I'm moving closer," Rory said.

Since he didn't order her to stay put, Eden didn't. When he started to belly-crawl closer to Helen, so did she. If this took a turn for the worst, she wanted to be by his side to help him.

Rory kept his attention pinned to his aunt, and Eden continued to keep watch behind and around them. She also kept an eye out for IEDs, and that was a little easier to do with her face only inches from the ground.

She cringed when she saw another of those deep holes off to the side. Any minute now, there could be an explosion. Any minute, Rory and she could die.

Of course, living with that threat of possible death was part of the job, but they had so many reasons to live, and she hoped she got a chance to tell Rory how she felt about it. She promised herself then and there if they made it out of this alive, she wouldn't put up another barrier between them.

And she would tell him that she loved him.

For now, she had to push that thought away and keep moving.

They finally got close enough to Helen for them to see there was indeed tape around her torso and her neck. Her hand, too, the one holding the gun in place.

Had the killer done that so that they would see the

weapon and then shoot first, killing her? Or was this all Helen's doing? Maybe a way to try to make herself look innocent of the other murders since she was now seemingly a victim, too.

She was alive because Eden could see her chest moving. But her eyes were closed, and the woman definitely wasn't responding when they called out to her.

"I don't see any IEDs around her," Rory whispered.

"Neither do I."

Eden wasn't sure what to make of that. Again, if this was the killer's doing, then he or she hadn't staged the scene like Ike's.

There were differences in Mellie's and Brenda's stagings as well, with Brenda left at the back of the barn and Mellie's body toward the front. And Carter's murder was nothing like the other victims except for the cause of death. That's the only thing that all of them had in common.

They'd been stabbed and left to die.

As far as she knew, Ike hadn't been stabbed. Judging by the lack of blood, neither had Helen. So as far as Eden was concerned, both of them stayed on the list of potential suspects.

Eden thought back to the way Ike had been tied up against that tree, and that was something he could have done himself. Ditto for the head wound. It would have taken a lot of guts to hit himself on the head, but it might be a small price to pay to make himself look innocent.

And it was the same for Helen.

They had no idea if that tape went all the way around the tree so Helen could have posed herself this way and be lying in wait. A clever way to get them closer and kill them. Still, that didn't feel right. If the plan was to pin all of this on Ike, then why hit him and tie him up? Helen could have probably figured out a way to get him on scene, so he could be blamed for the latest attack.

Eden didn't voice that thought, and she continued to move with Rory, inch by excruciating inch. They were still a good ten feet away from Helen when Eden saw another of those holes in the ground.

Right in front of Helen.

If they'd charged toward her, they would have fallen in. Maybe landing right on an IED that would have then exploded.

"Frank!" someone shouted.

Eden groaned because she instantly recognized the voice. What the heck was she doing there?

Diedre.

"Frank," the woman shouted again.

Eden looked behind them to see Diedre running up the trail toward them. Bennie was right behind her, and he practically tackled the woman before she could get to Rory and her.

Diedre shrieked, and there was probably some pain that went along with the tackle. But Eden was glad Bennie had done that because they had no idea what the woman's intentions were.

"Where's Frank?" Diedre called out, her voice breaking into a sob. "Did Helen kill him?"

"Sorry," Bennie said. He was huffing and fighting to hang on to Diedre, who was trying to wriggle out of his grip. "I didn't see her until she started running right past me. She didn't drive up in a vehicle, and she must have cut her way through the woods, so Judson didn't spot her."

So Diedre had sneaked onto the scene, and Eden couldn't think of a single good reason for her to do that.

"Did Helen kill him?" Diedre repeated, and she was flat-out crying now.

Maybe it was an act, but if so, she was certainly putting a lot into it. Then again, she might need that effort to try to convince them she wasn't there to kill them.

"Why are you here?" Rory snapped.

"For Frank," Diedre said quickly. "I know he's here... somewhere."

"And how would you know that?" he asked.

"Because I put a tracker app on his phone," Diedre blurted, but then stopped and gasped as if she hadn't meant to say that aloud. "I, uh, I thought he was seeing Helen or someone else."

So...jealousy. Or a way to track him so she could kill him. But if so, then it was stupid of her to admit that she was tracking him.

"I went to his house, and when he wasn't there," the woman continued, "I used the tracker, and it led me here. To her," she spluttered, her gaze landing on Helen. There was rage in Diedre's eyes now. "Did you kill him?" she shouted to Helen.

"What makes you think Frank is dead?" Eden asked.

"There was blood on his porch. So he's been hurt. She hurt him and brought him here to kill him the way she did Brenda and Mellie," Diedre said.

Rory was quick to respond to that. "You're certain Helen killed them? You have proof?"

"No, but she did it," Diedre snarled. "She must have so she could set up Ike."

Diedre's gaze met Eden's, and suddenly the woman didn't seem so certain of that. Again, it could all be an act, but there seemed to be some doubt now.

"Oh, God," Diedre muttered, her gaze slashing to her

left, where there were more of those clustered cedar trees. "Frank?" The sobbing came to a quick halt, and there was shock coating both her voice and her face.

Eden was still on her belly, but she automatically turned in that direction, too, bringing up her gun. Beside her, Rory did the same. And they both took aim at Frank, who stepped out from behind one of the trees.

He didn't have a gun, but there was something else in his hand. Something that Eden knew could kill them all.

Frank was holding an IED.

RORY BOLTED TO his feet, getting in a firing stance.

But he didn't have a safe shot.

Not with Frank's fingers on what Rory was pretty sure was the detonator of that IED he was holding.

"This ends here," Frank said, glancing at all of them. "It'll end for Ike, too, since he'll be blown to bits in ten minutes or so. Those IEDs are all on timers. And there won't be enough time for the bomb squad to get in here and defuse them."

Rory silently cursed. So Frank was cleaning house. Or rather, that was his plan, anyway, but Rory didn't intend to let that plan come to fruition. Somehow, he had to stop this.

But how?

And why had Frank gone off the deep end like this?

Diedre had started sobbing again, and she was muttering stuff that Rory couldn't make out. But she wasn't the only one making sounds. So was Helen. She was moaning, regaining consciousness.

"Rory?" Judson shouted. "What the devil is going on?" He was running toward them, but pulled up when he saw the answer to his own question.

All hell was about to break loose.

"What will it take to get you to put down that IED and surrender?" Rory asked Frank.

Frank laughed, but there was no humor in it. In fact, just the opposite. He groaned, the sound of a man in emotional agony. Rory didn't have a shred of sympathy for him, though, since he was looking at the face of a killer.

"No surrender," Frank muttered. "This ends now." And he shifted the IED as if ready to set it off.

Think. Think fast. Rory had to do something.

"At least tell us why we're dying," Rory insisted. "You can do that much for us. We deserve answers."

Frank seemed to consider that, and Rory could feel the seconds ticking by. He had no idea how much firepower was in those IEDs around Ike, but it was possible they'd blow up the entire area. If that was the case, though, then Frank likely wouldn't be holding yet another IED. Unless that was insurance that they all die.

Frank included.

But maybe that had been his plan all along.

"I didn't mean for Mellie to die," Frank finally said. "That was an accident. She'd seen Ike and me fighting at my wife's grave, and she came to my ranch to check on me. I didn't hear her when she drove up, and she walked right in to my workshop. She saw me making one of these." He lowered his gaze to the IED. "She knew what it was, and she turned to run. I caught her, and, I, uh, had a knife in my hand that I was using to strip some wires..." His voice trailed off.

"And you murdered her," Eden said, finishing his sentence. "You murdered her!"

Rory could only imagine the firestorm of emotions that she was feeling right now. Frank had killed her foster mother, and it didn't matter that he'd just called it an accident. Mellie was dead. So were Lou Garcia, Brenda and Carter. Garrison had nearly been killed, too.

And Frank had clearly tried to cover his tracks.

Clearly taken steps to prevent him from being ID'ed as the killer. The CSIs had found no IED-making equipment during their search, so that meant Frank had cleaned up that area and had obviously moved his IED factory elsewhere.

"No," Diedre sobbed. "No, please say this isn't true."

Everyone, including Frank, ignored her, and from the corner of his eye, he could see Judson easing back a few steps. Rory doubted the deputy was trying to distance himself from the blast, though. No. He was likely trying to get to Ike to see what he could do about saving him.

"Did Brenda walk in on you, too?" Eden snapped. "Did you kill her by accident as well?"

Frank didn't react to the anger. "No," he said with an eerie calmness, "but Mellie had apparently called her to tell her what had happened at the cemetery with Ike, and she told Brenda that she was coming to see me."

So there was the motive for two murders. Heck, for framing Ike as well, since it was obvious now that the altercation at the cemetery had been what set Frank off. That had caused him to snap, and this was the result.

But there was something about this that didn't make sense.

"There was five months between Mellie's and Brenda's murders," Eden pointed out. "That's a long time to wait to tie up any loose ends."

Frank nodded. "Brenda kept asking me about Mellie, kept bringing up the visit that Mellie told her she was going to make to see me. I think Brenda was looking for evidence to prove that I'd been the one to kill her. Playing detective," he grumbled under his breath.

"Brenda never said anything to the cops about Mellie's plans to visit you," Rory informed Frank.

"Because I told her that Mellie hadn't come," Frank admitted, "and I turned the tables on her by saying that Mellie had told me that she was going to see her, to see Brenda. So it was sort of an impasse. I wouldn't tell on Brenda, and she wouldn't tell on me. But I couldn't risk Brenda staying quiet forever. So I asked her if I could meet her at her house to discuss it. She agreed."

Frank stopped again. Rory didn't know how much of those ten minutes were gone now, but each second counted.

"I drugged Brenda, planted those burner phones, took her to the barn. And I killed her," Frank admitted. "At least I thought I had. When I left her, I believed she was dead."

"But you set an IED just in case," Eden snapped. "An IED that killed a CSI."

"I'm sorry about that. He wasn't meant to die. But I wanted to bring down the whole damn barn because I thought it was over. I thought Ike would be blamed for Brenda's death, and that he'd end up rotting in jail. But you didn't arrest him," he practically shouted. "He was a free man, walking around, continuing to spread his hatred. Not paying for the misery he brought to my life."

Rory didn't voice the reason for that misery. It wasn't just the incident in the cemetery, but the fact that Ike had had an affair with Frank's wife. A wife he had obviously loved.

"It was supposed to be over," Frank continued, his voice lower now. And he was too composed, considering what he had done. Considering what he was about to do. "But

Carter had taken some pictures of me going into Brenda's house that night, and he tried to blackmail me with them."

"And you killed him, too," Rory concluded. "Three. That's makes you a serial killer."

Frank didn't have time to react to that because Diedre spoke before he could say anything.

"But I saw blood on your porch," the woman said, like some kind of plea to help her make sense of this. "I saw it and thought you'd been hurt or killed."

Frank shook his head and tipped his head to his arm. "I cut myself when I was moving some of the IEDs."

So no one had harmed him. Not physically, anyway.

"You son of a bitch," Helen yelled. She was conscious now, and she had her narrowed eyes pinned on Frank. "I trusted you. I was in love with you. And this is how you repay me? You asked me to meet you so you could give me proof that Diedre had murdered Mellie and Brenda."

"What?" Diedre howled.

A surge of anger must have gone through Diedre because she tried to get up. No doubt to charge at Frank so she could try to have a go at him. Bennie, thankfully, shut that down by wrapping his arms around the woman and holding on tight.

"I wasn't going to pin the murders on you," Frank insisted, sparing Diedre a dismissive glance. "In fact, you weren't even supposed to be here. You were supposed to… live," he muttered.

"But I was supposed to die?" Helen snapped. She was struggling to get out of the tape restraints, and she was succeeding. Rory only hoped the gun wasn't loaded, because if she tried to shoot Frank, he'd set off the IED. "Why did you lump me with Mellie, Brenda and Carter? I wasn't blackmailing you. I didn't know you were a killer."

"You're insurance," Frank said. "Ike's fingerprints are on the tape and gun. After this is over, the CSIs would have found that. They would have found his prints on some of the IEDs, too. And the equipment to make the IEDs is in the cargo bed of his truck. There's a note back at my house, saying that I learned that Ike was going to kill you and that I came here to try to stop him."

Rory cursed. "But Ike would have been dead."

He nodded. "Dead, but always remembered as a cold-blooded killer. That's the legacy I want for him. The legacy he deserves."

"And what legacy do you deserve?" Rory snapped to get his attention. "You're killing innocent people."

Much to Rory's surprise, Frank seemed to consider that, and he looked at Diedre. "There's a big hole from the old mineral springs right in front of Helen. Get in it now. You, too," he added, spearing Eden with his intense gaze. "And Bennie. It might protect the three of you from the blast."

Rory didn't even have to think about this. "Go," he ordered Diedre, Bennie and Eden.

Bennie and Diedre quickly moved toward the hole. So did Helen, who had managed to get out of the tape. Eden didn't. Damn it. She stayed put.

"I'm not leaving you to die," she said, and then she added something that perhaps stunned them both. "I'm in love with you."

Despite everything, Rory managed a brief smile. Those were words he'd waited a long time to hear. And to say.

"I'm in love with you, too," he told her. Now, he had to play dirty. He had to say or do whatever it took to save her. "I need you to stay alive for Tyler. He can't lose both of his parents. Our son needs you."

She shook her head. "He needs you, too. I need you," Eden added.

"This ends now," Frank repeated in a mutter.

Rory knew the man meant it, and moving as fast as he could, he hooked his arm around Eden, diving toward that hole with her in tow.

Behind them, the blast ripped through the air.

Chapter Eighteen

Eden wasn't sure if Rory or the blast had propelled them into the hole. Maybe a combination of both. But they landed on top of Bennie, Diedre and Helen.

It wasn't exactly a cushioned fall, since bodies slamming against bodies was rough, and Eden saw stars when her elbow rammed against the rock wall. And she couldn't breathe. The air was gone, and her lungs were clamped into a vise.

She wasn't the only one, either. All of them were gasping, and Eden thought that maybe the IED had created some kind of vacuum. Still, the fact that she could feel the pain meant she was alive.

She turned—well, as much as she could turn in the small space—and saw Rory. He was right behind her. Alive, too, thank goodness. They had survived. But were they out of danger?

Dragging in some much needed air, Eden looked at the others, and in a blink, she knew there was no threat here. Diedre was trying to scream, and she was clinging to Bennie. Helen was groaning, the sound of raw pain, and Eden realized the gun still taped to her hand had apparently gouged into her left arm. The barrel had been rammed into her skin.

Eden unraveled the rest of the tape, checking to see if the gun was loaded. It wasn't. Then she checked the wound. It was bleeding. Not a fatal injury, but she'd need medical attention. Heck, they all would.

"Ike," Rory blurted on a gasp of breath.

That put her heart right back in her throat, and the images flashed like neon signs in her head. Ike with all those IEDs around him. And Judson had gone back to try to help him.

Rory caught on to the top of the hole, and he levered himself out, his gaze sweeping around. He'd managed to hold on to his gun. Unlike Eden. She had to pick hers up from the bottom of the hole.

"I'll go check on Judson and Ike," Rory insisted.

She'd had no doubts that was his plan, but Eden crawled out with him, and she glanced around at the disaster Frank had created. There was rubble everywhere, along with his body. Or rather, what was left of it. He was dead, and she was glad of it. Mellie's killer had finally gotten the justice he deserved.

Too bad he'd hurt and killed so many other people in the process.

Eden whirled back toward Rory, who had started to move toward Ike. She moved, too, ready to help.

But she didn't get the chance.

There was another blast, even louder than the other one, and it shook the very ground beneath them. She saw the sickening dread go over Rory's face. Felt the same emotion in every part of her body.

And they took off running.

They could have an officer down. Judson could be seriously injured. Or worse. They had to get to him and Ike.

The adrenaline gave them a boost of speed, and they

sprinted toward the spot where they'd left Ike. There wasn't much left of it. The cedars had all been ripped apart like giant toothpicks, and there was a huge hole in the ground.

But no bodies.

"Here," someone called out.

Judson. She whirled around and saw the deputy near one of the cruisers. And he wasn't alone. He had Ike with him. He'd saved Rory's father.

Rory didn't take off running. Instead, he looked down at the ground, no doubt checking for more IEDs. That slowed them down considerably, but they eventually made it to Judson and Ike. Like Rory and her, they were both gasping for breath, while Arnette looked on in horror from the cruiser.

"Frank's dead," Rory informed them. "He confessed to everything."

Later, there'd be a ton of reports to do. Witness accounts needed to be taken, and the whole scene would have to be examined, but for now, they all just stood there a moment, trying to come to terms with the nightmare they'd just escaped.

"How'd you get Ike to safety?" Rory asked Judson.

"I circled behind him. No IEDs there. So I got him loose, and we got the hell out of there as fast as we could."

"Barely escaped," Ike muttered, using his forearm to wipe away the blood on his head.

"You and Helen need an ambulance," Eden finally said.

"It's on the way," Judson assured her, and there were indeed the sounds of sirens in the distance. He opened his mouth, probably to ask about Bennie, but he stopped, motioning toward Bennie, Helen and Diedre, who were all making their way toward them.

Neither of the women was saying anything, which meant

the shock had likely set in. After the shock, well, there'd be a lot of emotional turmoil. But they were alive, and Eden figured that reminder would be setting in soon as well. They'd all gotten lucky and were here despite Frank's sick plan of revenge.

The irony of that plan was Ike was alive, too, and he wouldn't be rotting in jail as Frank had wanted.

Arnette finally got out of the cruiser, went straight to Ike and taking him by the arm, he looked at Rory. "I'd like to get my client out of here and take him to the ER. Any objections?"

Rory looked at his dad. "You could go in an ambulance." He tipped his head as it came into sight.

"I'd rather go with Arnette." But he didn't budge. Ike just stood there a couple of moment. "Thanks for saving my life," he muttered, glancing at Judson, Rory and, yes, even at Eden.

The three of them muttered some variations of "you're welcome." And they meant it. Despite Ike being a despicable human being, he hadn't deserved to die, though Eden hoped he'd learned a lesson about taunting a man over his wife's grave.

"You're going to owe my client an apology," Arnette snapped, clearly stepping back into his lawyer role.

"Shut the hell up, Arnette," Ike told him, and he headed toward the Jag with the lawyer trailing right along behind him.

Eden was finally ready to take a breath to try to tamp down some of this adrenaline, but then Rory spoke.

"Put Helen in the ambulance," Rory instructed Judson. "There might be other IEDs."

Sweet heaven. Eden hoped that wasn't true, but as enraged as Frank had been, there could be more.

"Go in the ambulance with her to the hospital," Rory added to Judson. "And take a statement from her if you can."

After Judson gave him a nod, Rory shifted to Diedre, who looked on the verge of starting that shrieking again. "Where are you parked?"

She motioned toward a trail up the road.

"Don't go there," Rory ordered her. "Get in the cruiser with Bennie. He'll take you to the station, and after the bomb squad has cleared the area, someone will bring you your car. Oh, and FYI, it's against the law to put a tracker on someone's phone. You're lucky it didn't lead you to getting killed."

Diedre didn't shriek, but she started to sob as Bennie led her to the cruiser. Eden doubted they'd actually file charges against Diedre, especially since they had so many other loose ends to wrap up. For starters, checking for IEDs and recovering the explosive-making equipment that Frank said he'd put in Ike's truck. The bomb squad would see to that, and then the CSIs and ME would have to come in. It could take days to clean up this crime scene.

"I want to see Tyler," Eden said simply.

He nodded, and he motioned for her to move into the cruiser with him. "So do I. We can leave as soon as the bomb squad gets here."

Good. Because holding their son might start untangling this mass of nerve.

She slid into the passenger's seat and did something else to start that untangling. Eden reached over and pulled Rory to her.

Yes, instant relief.

Along with so many other feelings. Not the nerves. No, this was something much stronger.

"I'm not taking it back," she told him while they clung to each other.

"Taking what back?" he asked.

"That *I love you*. I meant it, and I'm not going to claim it was part of the fear or adrenaline surge."

Rory eased back from her, a slow smile forming on his mouth. A mouth he promptly used to kiss her. An incredible kiss that worked wonders. The nightmare of the attack didn't exactly vanish, but the kiss put a serious dent in it.

When he eased back, Rory was still smiling. "I'm not taking it back, either. I'm in love with you, Eden, and no, that wasn't the adrenaline talking. That was all me."

"Ike is never going to approve of us being together," she reminded him. And she returned the favor by giving him one of those scalding kisses.

Rory didn't even attempt to end the kiss so he could respond. He just kissed and kissed and kissed, until he stirred up a ton of heat inside her.

"Ike has no say in…us," he said. "This love is between you and me. And Tyler," he added.

Now, she smiled. Because, yes, Tyler was in on this, too.

The weight just lifted off her heart. Weight that felt as if it'd been there for a very long time. Eden suddenly felt as if everything was going to be fine.

Better than fine, she amended.

Everything was finally going to be *right*.

* * * * *

Look for more books in
New York Times *bestselling author*
Delores Fossen's miniseries, Renegade Canyon,
coming soon from Harlequin Intrigue!

Harlequin Reader Service

Enjoyed your book?

Try the perfect subscription for Romance readers and get more great books like this delivered right to your door.

See why over 10+ million readers have tried Harlequin Reader Service.

Start with a Free Welcome Collection with free books and a gift—valued over $20.

Choose any series in print or ebook.
See website for details and order today:

TryReaderService.com/subscriptions